"Wicked" Women 101

"Wicked" Women 101

Susanna Carr

BRAVA

KENSINGTON PUBLISHING CORP.
http://www.kensingtonbooks.com

BRAVA BOOKS are published by

Kensington Publishing Corp.
850 Third Avenue
New York, NY 10022

All Kensington titles, imprints and distributed lines are available at special quantity discounts for bulk purchases for sales promotion, premiums, fund-raising, educational or institutional use.

Special book excerpts or customized printings can also be created to fit specific needs. For details, write or phone the office of the Kensington Special Sales Manager: Kensington Publishing Corp., 850 Third Avenue, New York, NY, 10022. Attn. Special Sales Department. Phone: 1-800-221-2647.

Brava and the B logo Reg. U.S. Pat. & TM Off.

ISBN 0-7582-0828-6

First Kensington Trade Paperback Printing: January 2005
10   9   8   7   6   5   4   3   2   1

Printed in the United States of America

"Six Weeks to Sensuality"

To Lori Foster, who had faith in this story's potential and gave me a boost of confidence when I needed it the most. Thanks.

Special thanks to Jesse Petersen, who didn't mind my follow-up e-mails and phone calls that put her psychology degree to the test. Her enthusiasm made the research bearable. Any mistakes are mine alone.

"Code Pink"

To my twin sister, who can now stop bugging me about when I'm going to dedicate a story to her.

"Fantasies Are Forever"

To Jane and Sinclair, who always listen to my ideas with straight faces, who are brave enough to talk to me on my bad days, and who encourage me to grab for my dreams.

Contents

Six Weeks to

Sensuality

Chapter 1

The high-pitched beep alerted him.

Dr. Marc Javier glanced distractedly at his computer. The reminder box slowly appeared on the screen like a sleepy sunrise.

Claim Amy Bryce today.

Energy whooshed through his body with a force that left his breath staggering in his lungs. A very masculine smile slowly tugged at his mouth as he stared at the message. Primitive hunger licked his blood as the call of the hunt echoed deep in his psyche.

After all this time, he was finally allowed to act. With slow, deliberate moves, Marc rose from his chair. "Thank you, Kayla," he murmured to his research assistant. "I'll check back with you later today."

Kayla's head jerked up. "Sir?"

"I'm sure you can handle any problems that come up."

"You want me in charge of the Reclaim Your Sensuality project today? But, Dr. Javier, this is a crucial—"

"No time like the present." He walked around his desk and helped her out of her seat.

She gulped and waved around the printouts. "But to see if it supports your hypothesis—"

"You'll do fine." He guided her to the door.

"—of being a more effective intimate communicator—"

Marc shut the door on her ramblings and walked back to his desk. He was too focused on his strategy, one that he'd spent a great deal of time and effort in developing. He had done the calculations. Considered the variables and worst-case scenarios. Consulted the institute's schedule, his horoscope and hers. Had he known Amy's cycles, he would have included that in the equation.

And all the while, he had waited impatiently for this moment. It had been a monumental achievement not to cast his plans to the side and claim his mate immediately.

But today was the day. Amy was physically, mentally and psychologically primed to accept him.

To be his.

Not accept him as some transitional man or get-back-at-the-world fling. But to accept him as her one and only.

Marc shoved his worn T-shirt into his faded jeans. When he noticed the tremor in his hands, he stopped and curled his fingers. He only had one chance to get this right. Catch Amy at the wrong moment, say the wrong thing, and the tenuous friendship they had built would snap.

Taking that into consideration, maybe he should wait another hour, when she got off work. He checked the clock. True, he might risk getting there after she left, but her blood sugar would be low and he could supply her with her favorite red licorice.

Another beep penetrated his mind. He turned back to the computer screen.

Do it now!

Marc rolled his eyes. He hated when he did that to himself. He left his office before he suffered through any more reminders.

When he exited the building, the Illinois heat slapped him head-on, but Marc didn't flinch. He breathed the scent of freshly mowed grass as he crossed the institute's courtyard to the library.

While his body crackled with energy, his brain bellowed "Caution! Caution!" With all the mixed messages rattling through his body, it was amazing he was upright and walking.

The significance of what he was about to do came crashing upon him as he reached the entrance to the library.

Recklessness singed his veins. His self-discipline was dancing along the line between control and chaos. If that didn't give him a buzz, nothing would.

But nothing could go wrong. He had prepared for this with military precision. With a renewed confidence, he surged into the library and immediately saw Amy Bryce as she stepped out of the archive office.

Marc felt a heady rush as he watched her brown hair shimmer in the sunlight. The sensations amplified when he noticed how her loose dress skimmed and hinted at the curves underneath.

"Amy!" Marc was immediately shushed by the front desk matron. He lowered his voice. "Can I talk to you for a moment?"

Amy's face brightened. "Dr. Javier."

"Marc," he corrected. It was always the same exchange, and he found the ritual strangely intimate.

"Marc," she said in a husky voice. She pressed her lips together as if the word was forbidden. "I'm sorry, but I have to—"

"It will just take a minute." A life-altering minute filled with promise, but she might not see it that way.

Stop it. Positive attitude. Visualize success.

"Amy, I want . . ." He frowned. "Amy?" He wanted her attention, for one thing. That was crucial. But from the look on her face, it was obvious something more fascinating behind him had captured her attention.

She looked like she was in a stupor, Marc decided. Maybe the licorice bribery would have been a smart move.

He reluctantly cast a glance over his shoulder. Blood roared into his ears as he watched Amy's ex-boyfriend walk through the main entrance holding a huge bouquet of long-stemmed roses.

His stomach did a free fall. Okay, this was bad. This was really bad. He hadn't predicted this type of intrusion. He honestly didn't think Kevin had the brainpower to realize what a mistake he'd made in breaking up with Amy.

But now he had. And Marc was too late. No! Almost too late. He whirled his attention to Amy. Her mouth gaped open, which was a first. Marc couldn't remember the last time she was caught unaware.

All of his plans were unraveling right before his eyes. His chest felt like it was imploding on itself. He couldn't panic. He had to do something before Kevin walked . . .

Right past them.

Marc looked at Amy with bewilderment. What was going on? She dipped her head, but she wasn't able to conceal the glow of stark pain in her eyes.

His first instinct was to shield Amy from Kevin. Protect her from the guy who she'd spent five years with and now didn't notice her when they were in the same room.

He knew that had to tear her up inside. Amy's pride was as deep as her loyalty. And because he knew that, Marc was determined not to show her pity. She would hate him for it.

"Ooh . . . something's up," the front desk librarian whispered loudly. From the corner of his eye, Marc saw the woman punch her male coworker in the arm.

"Eh?" The burly librarian didn't look up from his computer. "What are you talking about?"

"All day someone has been getting a rose delivered to her desk." Marc sensed the woman leaning over the wood counter to get a better view of Kevin heading for the elevator. "One perfect red rose on the hour, every hour."

Marc's eyes never left Amy's profile. Her face shook as she fought for composure. Admiration welled up inside him—and also the urge to tell her she didn't have to put on a brave face in front of him.

"Something is definitely up," the other librarian muttered as he typed.

Marc cleared his throat. "Amy?" He reached for her.

"Excuse me, Marc." His voice spurred her into action. "I have to run." She skittered out of his reach and went straight to the stairwell.

He dropped his outstretched arm as she pushed a heavy metal door. He'd miscalculated, Marc realized as he watched Amy escape. He was five minutes too late.

Marc let out a shaky exhale. No. He was five *years* too late.

Amy sprinted up the first flight of steps and her ribs complained from the unexpected exertion. Or maybe from the unexpected situation. It wasn't every day that she saw her ex-boyfriend bearing flowers. But, then, the roses weren't for her.

She stumbled against a step as her mind replayed Kevin walking through the library entrance. He worked in Administration and never stepped foot in the library if he could help it, claiming the dusty books made his allergies flare up.

The sheaf of red roses he held in his arms should have been giving him watery eyes and a sneezing fit. Instead those baby blues had sparkled with anticipation as he walked right by her. Amy winced at the memory. Right. By. Her.

And all in front of the very yummy Dr. Marc Javier. Her wince deepened. She had never stood a chance with the sexy scholar in the first place, but being invisible in front of her recent ex wasn't exactly a stellar recommendation.

The sting metamorphosed into raw power and she shot up the second flight of stairs. She had to get to the top floor before Kevin did.

And who did he think he was to look that good? Ex-boyfriends weren't supposed to look perfect, Amy decided. She stopped on the next landing, huffing and puffing. They were supposed to look like they were on the brink of insanity for losing women who were too good for them.

But Kevin didn't look like he'd been suffering. His blinding white smile did wonders for his pretty-boy face. The same smile that used to make her heart skip a beat. Now she just wanted to rip it off his face and stomp on it a few times.

Stretching to the side, Amy tried to get rid of the hitching pain and glanced down at her faded denim jumper dress and scuffed, sensible shoes. She almost understood why Kevin didn't see her. Almost.

"Something is definitely up." Amy repeated the other librarian's prediction. Something Amy didn't want to know about. Her stomach twisted with dread as she hurried up the last flight of stairs.

Kevin was undoubtedly on his way to Tanya, who worked in the library director's office—the same office Amy had to report to immediately, thanks to an inopportune summons from the director.

She glanced at her watch, wondering if she could stall the meeting with her boss. No, Amy decided, and gritted her teeth in exasperation. It was too close to quitting time.

But she could do without seeing Kevin give Tanya the flowers. The two had treated her and the entire staff with more than enough public displays of affection.

She needed to run at supersonic speed if she wanted to get out of range before Kevin stepped out of the elevator.

Amy frantically peered out of the stairwell door and saw no one around. She bolted to the library director's office. Her heart felt like it was going to burst when she got to the office door and whipped it open.

She was too late.

Amy watched in horror as Kevin knelt before Tanya. Her brain deciphered the image in slow motion. The blood-red roses lay on the clean desk next to the crystal vase holding similar flowers. The blond goddess sat primly on her chair, her red miniskirt stretching tightly across her toned thighs. Kevin's infatuated expression was at level with Tanya's impressive breasts. He slid a more-than-two-months-pay diamond ring on her manicured hand.

"Will you marry me?"

Amy braced herself for her body to shatter. But she didn't feel a thing. Not a slap or a pinch from the words. Her body was numb. The serene, friendly expression was already in place. Amy was grateful that the ladylike image she lately fought hard for was automatic for this emergency.

"Yes, I will," Tanya declared. She grabbed Kevin's face with both hands and gave him an exuberant kiss. No one could miss how the engagement ring captured the fluorescent overhead light just so.

The office workers awed and clapped as the couple devoured each other's mouths with slurping, moaning sound effects. Amy wanted to throw up.

No, she wanted to throw a temper tantrum. Not just any kind of tantrum. An ear-blistering, plate-tossing, crying buckets, throw-yourself-onto-the-floor-and-give-a-good-howl temper tantrum.

But she had too much pride to indulge in such a public display. She'd wait until she got home.

Kevin came up for air, the red smear of lipstick staining his mouth. As he pulled away, he saw Amy by the door. He blanched and rose cautiously. Tanya turned to see what had captured Kevin's attention. Her brow puckered with irritation, but Amy noted the gleam of triumph in the woman's eyes.

"Amy," Kevin breathed out. The single word was laced with surprise and guilt with a healthy dose of caution.

The clapping evaporated instantly. The tension flashed and held in the room as she felt everyone watch her. Amy knew she had to make the first move. She hated being put in that position. Hated Tanya and Kevin for making a spectacle out of her.

She didn't understand why everyone was holding their breath, waiting to see what she did. Had she ever caused a scene in all of her twenty-seven years? For some reason, she inherited the unwanted role of playing the lady. She understood the benefits of meeting expectations. And she saw the disadvantages of breaking the rules.

Amy never broke the rules.

She walked up to the couple. "Congratulations, Kevin. Tanya." She fought to give them eye contact and succeeded. But she instinctively knew she needed to add something to the generic best wishes. "The two of you make a perfect couple."

Okay, that hurt, Amy decided as her smile stayed intact. Why had she said that? The gossips were going to analyze it for sure.

Kevin's shoulders relaxed. "Thank you." He placed a proprietary hand on Tanya's shoulder.

"Oh, thank you, Amy." Tanya's smile took on a hard edge. "That's so very kind of you. Are you sure you're not sore about all this?" She covered Kevin's hand with her own, and the diamond ring gave a sly wink.

"Of course not." Amy knew that would make Tanya's day. The woman had hated her at first sight and she reciprocated the feeling. Only she kept quiet about it. "Why would I be?"

Tanya didn't answer and Amy decided the woman was smarter than she looked. She knew better than to dredge up old history in front of an audience. "You'll come to our engagement party, won't you?"

Kevin's I'm-king-of-the-world smile slipped a notch. "Now, Tanya, we haven't even set it—"

"Of course," Amy answered recklessly, pride spurring her on. "I wouldn't miss it for anything."

Have you lost your mind? a little voice screamed inside

her. Why didn't she stop while she was ahead? What possessed her to volunteer for that brand of torment? She would rather eat dirt.

Amy's best friend Nicole was suddenly at her side. "Kevin, Tanya, how exciting!" Nicole gushed as she discreetly nudged Amy away from the desk. "Let me see that ring."

Amy gratefully edged back to the wall. She wanted to bolt out of the room and never return. She would wait for another well-wisher—no, maybe two more—and sneak out.

The library director hurried into the office. "Tanya, fax this for me, will you?" The older man suddenly noticed the small group around the secretary's desk. "Why is everyone standing around?"

"Kevin just popped the question to Tanya," Amy said, wishing her automatic response would take a hike. Being a lady was one thing; being a glutton for punishment was quite another. "And she accepted."

The library director's eyes lit up. He was a family man who found pleasure in weddings and births. And like most people in the small Midwestern town, he preferred if they fell in that order. "This calls for a celebration." He rubbed his hands. "Okay, everyone to the break room."

Great. Amy felt her shoulders sag and immediately straightened them. She had a good twenty minutes before she could leave. Any time before and everyone would know that her pride had taken a beating. Any time after and the muscles she used for smiling would atrophy. Those very same muscles were already trembling and burning from exertion.

Nicole wandered over to her as the rest of the office circled around Tanya's desk. "How are you doing?" she asked from the side of her mouth.

"How does it look like I'm doing?" she asked through her smile.

"You look like you're happy for the blessed couple." Nicole rolled her eyes.

"Oh, good. I was worried I had the deer-caught-in-the-headlights expression going."

"How are you really doing?" Nicole leaned against the wall and crossed her arms.

Amy wished she could copy the same stance, but the arm-crossing would make it look like she was sulking. "I'm fine." Her answer depressed her. Why couldn't she even tell her best friend the truth? Something was seriously wrong with her.

"Then you have nerves of steel. If I stumbled into watching my ex-boyfriend making a lavish production of proposing to my most hated enemy, I would be freaking out."

"I am freaking out," Amy confessed. She had no idea this was coming. She would have prepared herself. She would have taken the day off.

Her friend flashed a disbelieving look. "Then you don't freak out like a normal person."

Something flinched inside her. "I'll take that as a compliment."

"Why don't you bail out of here?" Nicole asked as she studied her pale, blank face with concern. "Go to the bar and get sloppy."

"That's unnecessary." And too risky. She couldn't drown her sorrows in public. Couldn't be seen with a hangover.

"I think this is definitely one of those occasions." Nicole pushed the door open and motioned for her to leave.

Tempting. Oh, so tempting. "I can't."

"I know, I know. You have a rep to protect. I will cover for you." She grabbed at Amy's arm. "Now go." Nicole gave a sudden jerk.

Amy crossed the threshold in an attempt to keep from kissing the floor. She turned around just as Nicole closed the door in her face. She could only hope her exit was graceful. And unnoticed.

She held her chin up as she walked past the office and onto the library floor. *Engaged.* The word reverberated around her head as she sought privacy in the maze of bookshelves. Kevin was engaged. To Tanya, of all people!

How was she so blind? Amy zigzagged through the rows of shelves. When Kevin's professional reputation had been at stake because of alleged misconduct with a female employee under his authority, Amy had done everything in her power to clear his name.

She had done damage control by playing the rules and by using her image. Her campaign had been discreet and effective. And she had hated every minute of it.

But most important, she hadn't caused a scene. It was incredibly difficult as her suspicions grew. Kevin's claims of innocence became inconsistent and arrogant. Nevertheless, she stood by her man.

It was a relief when the matter was quietly dropped. Kevin's career was back on track, but not once did he appreciate her role in recovering his reputation.

No, he thought it was just an unfortunate blip in his promising career. The board of governors admired his work too much. Of course, it also helped that the female employee transferred to another department. Although Kevin would never say anything so obvious.

And he never said a word when the same female employee became an office worker for the library director. Based on his friends' recommendations.

Tanya. Amy leaned her head against a shelf, remembering what one of her sorority sisters had labeled the woman: the office slut.

Amy closed her eyes, fighting off the weariness that invaded her bones. Her friend Caroline explained that every company had one, especially institutes devoted to researching sexuality and relationships.

All Amy knew was that once Tanya had transferred, Kevin

had dumped Amy and moved in with Tanya. As if that didn't hurt. Her loyalty meant nothing to him. He would rather offend the institute than stay away from Tanya.

Amy shook her head. She couldn't believe what a fool she was. Couldn't believe how she was still a fool.

Today she'd walked in on a setup and let them open fire on her. A flower on the hour, every hour, designed to pique the coworkers' interest. Popping the question at work.

And now they needed people to be happy about the engagement. But why now? Amy pulled away from the bookshelf and paced the aisle, trying to figure it all out.

Was Kevin finally seeing through the sexual haze and realizing he was a victim of office politics? That he was missing out on key meetings and e-mails as the personnel brandished their own sense of justice?

Image was important around here. Obviously, Kevin and Tanya had had enough of offending the institute's sensibilities. They finally understood more could be achieved if they played by the rules.

Getting engaged and incorporating the institute into the romance and wedding plans were ways of restoring Kevin's popularity. But they were missing one key ingredient.

Realization hit her chest. Anger pricked her stomach.

She got it now. They needed her public consent.

Damn it. Amy kicked the bookshelf and silently accepted the pain spearing through her foot.

She really blew it. Amy shook her head in self-disgust. She had a chance to wreck Tanya and Kevin's plans, but no! She had to act like a well-bred lady.

Stupid. She kicked the bookshelf again.

Stupid. Stupid. Stupid.

Looking like a chump while Tanya flashed a triumphant smile as her engagement ring just happened to catch the light.

It was like Tanya was mocking her, secretly saying, "I

stole Kevin from you. You couldn't do anything about it. I won."

No, Amy thought, you got Kevin because he's an idiot.

Amy placed her fists on her hips and paced. Why screw around with you when he had me taking care of him and our home?

Why risk his reputation to be with you when his future was practically guaranteed if he stuck with me?

And why did she feel like she had lost something? She was over Kevin. So over. It had been months since he'd left her. They had already been close to ending it before the Tanya debacle. They had broken up by mutual agreement.

Okay, that wasn't entirely true. Kevin didn't want people to know he had walked out, so he said it was a mutual decision. And he knew Amy's pride wouldn't allow her to be seen as the discarded woman.

She snorted. Woman? Kevin didn't think so. "I will always care about you, Amy," he had said right before he'd walked out on her. "But it's different with Tanya. She's so sexy she makes my head spin. She's a goddess and you're . . . well, you're Amy."

The words played round and round in her mind as she covered her face with her hands. *You're Amy.* Sweet Amy. Sweet, loyal Amy with the word "sucker" tattooed on her forehead.

She's not woman enough. Not sexy enough. Not enough.

An arc of anger consumed her body. She lashed out, throwing the heavy volumes off the shelf with a fierce sweep of her hand.

The thunderous noise pierced the silence of the library. For once, Amy didn't care. She stepped over the books and marched out of the aisle.

Everyone knew it. Everyone knew she was not enough. She was tired of being not enough. Sick of being a lady. Sick and tired of coming in last. Of being lied to.

Because it was a lie. Good girls don't inherit the earth. Sluts do.

Marc watched silently behind the bookshelf as Amy stormed down the aisle. A smile of deep satisfaction wiped away his sulking scowl.

He uncurled and rose from his favorite chair in the library as a sense of excitement licked his blood. He knew it. He knew underneath Amy's ladylike demeanor there was fire.

Not that he had anything against her ladylike image, he decided as he watched Amy disappear through the maze of bookshelves. He admired how she mastered her emotions to achieve the cool beauty. He understood the difficulty behind every controlled movement.

Especially when it came to her ex-boyfriend. He remembered how much he had wanted to punch Kevin's face in when the scandal broke. How could that man have betrayed Amy? Marc wondered as he strode to the back stairs. How could he have taken her fidelity and loyalty for granted?

Marc knew those qualities were rare gifts. He appreciated the price the giver paid for it. It was one of the reasons he'd become a clinical psychologist specializing in relationships.

His stride slowed down as he noticed a familiar call sheet on the bulletin board next to the staircase. It was hard to miss the eye-catching, hot-pink paper that Kayla preferred, the words "Sensuality Project" shouting at him in big, bold letters.

Marc rolled his eyes. No wonder they had to turn away volunteers on a project about becoming an effective intimate communicator. He tore it from the board and was ready to crumple the paper just as Amy Bryce stormed around the corner. She looked stunning, Marc decided as she held herself together with barely controlled fury.

"Oh." She skittered to a stop and took a deep breath, trying to regain her cool composure. "Dr. Javier."

"Marc," he corrected, quietly disturbed when she said nothing. "How are you doing?" he asked gently.

She didn't seem to hear him. "What's that?" Amy took the paper from his hand. Intensity gripped her features.

"It's a call for my newest research project." He watched with growing fascination as her eyes glittered with certainty. Her jaw tilted up with determination.

"Where do I sign up?"

"Wh-what?" Amy wanted to participate in a sensuality project? With him in charge? No. No way. A thousand possible things that could go wrong bombarded his brain.

"It sounds interesting," she said coolly as she handed back the paper. "And you said you need volunteers."

He saw that look in her eye. His refusal was not an option. He cleared his throat with a shaky cough. "I don't need any more volunteers."

"Then drop one and let me take their place."

He met her gaze and held it. To his surprise, she did not look away. "Why is it so important?"

Her lips parted. He held his breath as she hesitated. Disappointment crashed through him as the vehement gleam in her eyes wavered. "It's not." She stepped back. "Dumb idea. Forget it."

Marc grabbed her wrist. She felt delicate underneath his large hand. "I don't need any volunteers for the control groups," he said, wondering what he was doing. He was following his gut instinct and doing everything he could not to let this opportunity escape. "But I do need someone for a . . . an experiment with this research project. Are you interested?"

"Yes," she replied without hesitation. "I'm in."

Chapter 2

She looked good in his lair.

Marc propped his elbow on the battered rolltop desk and covered his smile with his hand. He knew better than to stretch and relax like a smug tiger. He had just started the hunt, and if Amy knew what he was thinking, she would bolt like frightened prey.

He supported his chin with his hand and studied his quarry. Amy sat primly on the tattered burgundy settee, erasing madly on the questionnaire.

She didn't exactly blend in, he decided as he cast a look around the turmeric-yellow room. The weakening sunlight seeped through the window. Fat leafy plants bumped against the vivid watercolors scattered across the walls and trailed down the glassed-in legal bookcases.

Marc had been acutely aware of every move Amy made since she stepped into his small office half an hour ago. They agreed to meet in the evening after everyone went home, but now they were alone in the building and Marc wished he had a distraction before he did something stupid.

Amy wasn't a disruptive force of nature, but she possessed a quiet power that drew him in. She held his attention while giving his office the peace he had tried hard to achieve in the eclectic design.

Amy leaned back against the soft suede and glared at the survey. "Okay." She took a deep breath. "I'm done."

He reached for the pages that she offered. His fingers grazed hers. Every muscle in his body twanged like the soft sitar music in the background as his large fingers crimped the paper.

Marc drew away with great precision and studiously ignored the tension arcing over them. He swiped his eyeglasses off his desk and jammed them on his nose, hoping the wire rims wouldn't bend under his grip.

"Sit back and relax," he suggested to Amy, wondering if he could practice what he preached. He leaned back in his wooden office chair, which creaked incessantly. "Once I review this, we'll get started."

"Wait!" Her eyes bulged as her hand went up like a traffic cop. "You're going to go over that *now*? While I'm sitting here?"

"Yes." She looked stunned. Horrified. Any minute now she was going to curl up in a ball and hide. If she felt that way after answering questions, he didn't want to know how she was going to handle practical applications. "It will only take a moment," he promised.

She folded her arms across her chest and hunched her shoulders. "Don't you have a machine to take the score and spit out an analysis?"

"No." Why would she prefer a machine's opinion over his? He wondered about that as he scanned the questionnaire. Did she still feel that shy around him? He was determined that by the end of this sensuality project, she would find it no longer necessary to be wary of him.

She tapped her foot against the worn Persian carpet. "Nice office you have here. It's very . . . exotic."

He didn't glance up from the paper. "I spent a lot of time on the subcontinent researching polygamist marriages," he murmured as he skimmed through the biographical information that he already knew.

"Ah."

Her voice sounded faint to Marc as he reread the sensory section. Amy enjoyed public displays of affection and indulged in them often? Marc frowned at the box she checked. Since when? In the three years he had known her, he couldn't remember anyone touching her. And that included her ex-boyfriend.

Maybe she didn't know herself. He tugged off his eyeglasses and considered the possibility. Amy might think she indulged in public displays. Although how could someone make a mistake about that?

He glanced at her and watched the hectic color flush her cheeks. Her gaze skittered away. Amy nibbled the corner of her bottom lip.

Hmm . . . Marc bit the tip of his eyewear. *Curious.*

He flipped the page and reviewed the section designed to see how she chose her clothing through style, color and fabric. She checked the "bright eye-catching colors" box.

Marc blinked and read it again. He looked up and noted her gray T-shirt under her jumper.

Uh-huh. Okay. He continued reading.

Fabric? *Slinky.*

His forehead pleated into a deeper frown. Since when was durable cotton slinky?

Style? *Body conscious.*

His eyes flicked to the faded blue jumper that threatened to swallow her small form completely.

The only thing her body was conscious of was his suspicious looks. The pen she tapped at rapid speed was going to snap in half.

His annoyance blossomed as he scanned the remaining questions. "Interesting."

The pen stopped in midair. "It is?" Amy asked hesitantly.

"Yes." His clipped tone muzzled his irritation. "I had

no idea I had a budding nudist in my midst. According to this"—he gave the paper a crisp snap—"you sleep in the nude year round, skinny-dip if there is so much as a puddle in the vicinity and would rip off your shirt at the first sis boom bah."

Amy swallowed as her face grew pink. She opened her mouth and closed it again. "I, uh . . ." She shrugged. "I must have misunderstood the questions."

"Did you also misunderstand the food section? It says here," he read directly off the survey, "you frequently consume ice cream, cheese and chocolate for its thick, luscious texture."

"Yes." She gave a brisk nod. "What about it?"

His eyebrow rose a notch. "You and I both know that you are lactose intolerant."

Amy's eyelashes fluttered with surprise. "How did you know that?"

"When attendance is required at institute events, you learn a lot about your coworkers." Now was not the time to mention that he had noticed every little thing about her. "Explain this answer."

"What can I say?" She splayed her hands at her sides, frantically looking around the room for inspiration. Her face relaxed as she came up with an answer. "One always wants what one can't have."

Marc straightened in his chair. She wasn't going to fess up, huh? He was going to have to play hardball. "Then can you explain your answers in the sexuality section? Particularly the question in which you were supposed to check the scenarios you've participated in."

Her blush darkened. "I don't remember it offhand."

He looked at the questionnaire. "Some of the choices were anal, bondage, domination, exhibitionism, female-female sex, foot worship, male-male sex, leather, oral, orgy, solo, submission, tickling, threesomes, voyeurism and water sports."

"Mm-hmm?" The tips of her ears were beet-red.

He held out the paper and pointed at her answer. "You checked 'all of the above'."

Amy's complexion turned scarlet but she said nothing. Her eye contact wavered. Her need to break away was almost tangible.

"I'm trying to figure this out," Marc said in a slow, gentle voice, "so maybe you can explain it to me. How did you manage the male-male sex?"

Her pause hung endlessly. "I checked the wrong box."

"You think?"

She winced at his biting tone. "Can I have a do-over?"

"No." He tossed the survey aside. His eyeglasses landed on top of the papers. "What kind of person cheats on a sensuality test?"

"I wasn't cheating! I gave you what I thought were the right answers. And why do you have an 'all of the above' box if it doesn't make sense?" she added with righteous indignation.

"Amy, don't you understand?" He rubbed his eyes with the heels of his hands. "There are no right answers."

"Oh, please." She scrunched up her face. "That test is going to put me on a scale. I'm either frigid, average or a hedonist. And you know what? In sensuality, if you aren't a hedonist, you're a freak."

"That is not true." He rested his arms on his knees and leaned forward. "The only time sensuality should be a concern is when it holds you back from living your life fully. When you can't enjoy the life around you or when you enjoy it too much, then it's a problem."

"Okay, fine." She flopped back on the settee. "I get your point."

Marc knew her easy acquiescence meant she didn't want to discuss it further. "What is the point of taking this survey if you weren't going to answer it truthfully? Why even bother trying to be a part of this research project?"

She shifted uncomfortably. "You wouldn't understand."

He hesitated, reluctant to make the ultimatum. "You better make me understand, because as of this moment you're off the project."

Amy gasped with alarm. "You can't do that!"

He didn't want to do it, either, but he had no choice. "I can't have you jeopardizing my research."

Her shoulders sagged with guilt. "I wasn't trying to. I'm desperate, okay?" She raised her pleading eyes to meet his. "I *need* this sensuality makeover."

"Back up." He held up his hand. "This isn't a makeover. It's about reclaiming your sensuality."

"What if you're not sure you had it in the first place?" Her voice was a mere whisper.

"Come on, everyone has. Remember when you were a kid? Every day was a discovery? Every moment was a chance to get messy as you explored the physical world?"

"Not really." Her smile was wry. "My upbringing was in a very controlled, very academic environment."

He saw the concern behind the smile. The fear that maybe she wasn't sensual. That she would fail at this like she had presumably failed at everything sensual.

Marc knew there was no way he could use her as research now. But if he kicked her off the project, it would be a demoralizing blow to Amy. He rubbed the back of his neck and sighed. He couldn't do that to her. And, if he was being completely honest, he didn't want to destroy this opportunity he had with her.

Unless . . . A glimmer of an idea began to form. Unless he did the makeover and kept it out of the Reclaiming Your Sensuality project. And not let anyone know about it—especially Amy.

Amy would be furious if she found out any of this. But she didn't even know that he had created an experiment just for her and said it was a part of his research project.

Of course, that idea was now shelved, but not her participation. The only reason she had the courage to take part in the research was because she was helping out.

If she discovered she was his pro bono case, and one that had nothing to do with the project, he would be dead meat. But there was no way of her finding out. It was the perfect plan.

"I'll let you stay on," Marc said slowly as his mind searched for any hitch in the plan and found none, "only if you are completely honest from here on out."

"I will be," she vowed as she crossed her heart with her hand. "I swear."

"Good. One more thing before we start. Why are you doing this?" He didn't realize how much he wanted to know the answer until he asked.

"I want a change." She said it with straightforward simplicity. He could hear the determination behind it.

"I got that, but why now?"

Amy pressed her lips together. Marc waited patiently, knowing she wrestled over how much to reveal. She wanted to tell enough to convince him to keep her on the project, but not too much to use the information against her. He didn't like the idea that she couldn't trust him yet.

"I need to go to an engagement party."

She was going to have to do better than that. "Go on."

"My ex-boyfriend will be there." Her foot began to tap frenetically. "With his new fiancée. It's their engagement party."

"Mm-hmm." The old, familiar anger burned his stomach. So Kevin got engaged to someone else and Amy wanted to steal him away. The basic love triangle, only love never had anything to do with it.

"His fiancée is beautiful. No . . . sexy," she continued grudgingly. "And I need to"—she waved her hands— "to . . ."

"Compete," Marc finished in a brusque tone. He knew exactly what Amy wanted. It didn't matter who got hurt or what promises and vows were broken.

She thought about it and shook her head. "Well, not really. More like—"

"Win." She wanted to win back her man and was willing to use every means available. The fiery sensation in his stomach seeped to his chest and abdomen.

Amy frowned. She looked like she wanted to say something. Defend her goal? She changed her mind. "Okay, sure. I want to win. Do you think I can?"

He shouldn't judge her. After all, he stopped judging his parents long ago. His mom and dad embraced polyamory, or "many loves," with fervor. It had taken Marc a long time to understand why his parents had married and gotten involved in the swinging lifestyle.

Only when he was older did he understand that they craved the drama. They fed off the jealousies. When Marc did his graduate thesis on the swinging life, he found that some relationships thrived and flourished in that atmosphere. Others, like his parents, needed the drama.

Marc knew he wanted something different. Fidelity and trust were major points—ones he had stressed to his former wife when they got married. He thought his life was going to be different than the one which he'd grown up in.

That was, until he found his wife in bed with his business partner. On the analytical side, he could have broken it down as to why she chose to get caught, why she chose his business partner and why she chose that particular position she refused to do with him.

But he didn't feel analytical at that time. He felt all the rage, the hurt, the bitterness and the darkest emotions. The ones his parents relished every day. The ones he refused to live with for another moment.

It had been a good decision to divorce his wife and dissolve the medical practice with his friend. He was right to become a resident scholar at the institute. So what if he'd been here for three years with little to show for it, thanks to academic bureaucracy and politics? This was all a step toward the life he wanted. This was the kind of drama he could handle. Could master.

"Do you?" Amy repeated. "Do you think I can win?"

"It's possible," he answered hoarsely.

"Possible? Gee, thanks for the vote of confidence."

Marc shrugged, trying to rid himself of the insidious fire. "I don't know your competition."

"Yeah, you do," Amy said reluctantly. "Her name is Tanya. She was the employee who received special favors from Kevin."

Ouch. "I see." Marc kept his face passive so he wouldn't show the sympathy coursing through him. "Then it's time to get busy."

What the hell did she sign herself up for? Amy wondered as she looked around the institute's art garden. She wanted a transformation, not a psychology test. Especially not one that required her to look at art and tell Marc what she saw. What was up with that?

At least he didn't use those ink blot tests. Or make her run through a maze like a rat. But still, if you're going to ask a stupid question . . .

The whole exercise was stupid, Amy decided as impatience welled inside her chest. She didn't have time for these ridiculously cerebral Q&As. Amy wanted—no, needed—to skip steps, take shortcuts, and go straight to sensuality. Didn't Marc understand that?

She leaned against a metal structure that was still warm from the fading sun. This was so not her idea of a fun Friday night. And from the way Marc was knocking his forehead against the wooden sculpture, it wasn't his first choice, either.

"You're going to get a splinter if you keep doing that,"

Amy predicted as Marc knocked his forehead again. And again. And again.

She could see it now. *What did you do Friday night? I watched Marc give himself a concussion.* But, Amy had to admit, spending the evening with Dr. Marc Javier was something short of a miracle. The fact that it was not a hot date was a minor detail.

She folded her arms across her chest and studied Marc. Even when he butted his head with frustration, he looked sinfully sexy.

The guy didn't even know the full extent of his magnetism. Or he didn't see the need to work it. Why should he? His presence alone stopped traffic.

Her gaze traveled from his thick black hair curled in a haphazard fashion to the dramatic profile. His bronze face was comprised of severe angles and sharp slashes. His brown eyes were brilliant with intelligence and self-control. She sometimes wondered why he shielded them behind glasses. If he thought it diminished his allure, he was sadly mistaken.

She couldn't remember a time when he dressed formally. At work and fund-raising functions, it was basic casual wear. It suited him perfectly.

The simple white T-shirt he wore now neither flaunted nor hid the sculpted muscles. It beckoned a woman to slip her hands under the hem and palm the hot, taut skin underneath.

His jeans, however, embraced him like a lover. The soft denim clung to his compact muscles. The latent power of his hard thighs was evident.

He was a masterpiece, Amy decided, and sighed with regret. It was too bad that they were at that ambiguous place between acquaintances and friends. She knew it would never evolve to anything more, other than in her most secret fantasies.

Her skin prickled with awareness as the fragmented images swept through her mind. How many times had she been grabbed and imprisoned by those lean, authoritative hands in her Faceless Captor dream? Or when she saw his stunning face tighten with desire during the daydream when she danced for him at a scuzzy strip joint? She knew exactly how his eyes would grow hot with longing as she ripped her shirt off.

Amy pressed her thighs together as her abdomen grew heavy in response to the memories. All those fantasies and the hundreds of others had one recurring theme. Dr. Marc Javier. He had the dubious honor of starring in her erotic dreams. She always knew it was him, whether she couldn't see his face or whether he was a lust-crazed warlord determined to take her virginity.

But those fantasies were just that: fantasies. She'd had them for quite some time, never acted on them and never planned to. She certainly never told anyone, not even Nicole. What purpose would it serve? Nicole would point out that someone like Marc would never be attracted to someone like her.

Amy didn't need to be reminded. She knew how the world worked. But maybe things would change after her sensuality makeover.

"Okay." He moved away from the wooden sculpture. "Let's take this back to the beginning. We are here to exercise your sense of sight."

"Listen." She held up her hand and interrupted. There was no reason to prolong the exercise. "I am a patron of the arts. I have been to more museums than I care to admit."

"Glad to hear it," Marc said. Her pulse leaped as he approached her. "But this field trip isn't about interpreting the artist's intent. It's about what you see."

"The two are the same."

"Close, but not the same. When you interpret, you are recalling everything you learned in your art appreciation courses. You are making informed, analytical opinions about the artwork."

She slid him a look. "That's what you're supposed to do," she said with exaggerated patience.

"Not in this course. I want you to forget everything you learned. I will have you look at things differently."

Amy drew back as uneasiness coiled in her stomach. "I'm not sure I want to relearn everything." With the exception of her sexual allure quotient, she was doing just fine with what she knew now.

"You are making it harder than it is." He curled his hand around her arm and escorted her to another sculpture. His casual touch made her nerve endings jitter. "Tell me what you see with this sculpture."

"It's a stone artwork depicting a family," she said in a rush. She did her best to ignore the fact that his hand was inches away from brushing against her breast or that her nipples tightened with anticipation. "The female form is holding the child form, indicating that—"

"Stop, stop, stop." Marc released her as he fended off the summary with his hands. "You're telling me what the artist intends. When you look at it, what do you feel?" He motioned at the stonework.

She placed her hands on her hips and looked at the stone. "That it wasn't worth the hundred grand the institute paid for it."

His nostrils flared. "How would you describe it?"

"Vibrant. Alive. Flowing."

He glared at her with suspicion.

"Oh, all right." She huffed with exasperation. "That's what the art curator said about this piece."

"Do you automatically accept an expert's opinion?" His eyes gleamed with challenge.

"No. I'm still questioning the purchase of this artwork."

"How would you describe it to someone who knew nothing of art and she wasn't here?"

Amy shrugged. "It's a block of stone."

Marc's tight expression relaxed. "Okay, great. We're onto something here. Why did you mention the shape and the medium?"

Was the man obtuse? "Because it's a *block of stone*."

"I know that." Marc looked like his patience was holding on by a thread. "But why would you mention the shape instead of the size? Why didn't you mention that the stone was both smooth and rough?"

Because she didn't notice those things! She didn't question the texture or the size. It was a block of stone. Nothing more, nothing less.

"Because the stone is symbolic—"

He held his hand up to stop her. "I think we need a break." For a moment she wondered if he would thwack his head against the stone. Instead he glanced at his watch and relaxed instantly. "Yep, we have to hurry to the Arts Center or we'll be late."

Late? For what? Amy wondered. Another exhibit? Art appreciation used to be easier. She'd received perfect grades in her college art classes because she recalled what the experts said about the work. She'd read up on the artists and understood their underlying themes and interests.

"I'm giving you fair warning," Marc said as he led her across the brick courtyard. "You will not have a free lunch hour for the next few weeks."

Amy whimpered. Becoming sensual was hard work. "Why?"

"I'm making arrangements with the salon down the street. You will be there every Monday, Wednesday and Friday during your lunch hours. Hair, nails, whatever."

The whimper fizzled into something joyous. Cool! She'd be getting a makeover. She couldn't wait to be the "after." Hmm . . . that could be expensive. "I'm not sure I can afford that."

"It's taken care of," he said almost distractedly. "Don't worry about it."

Right. She forgot. Research projects got a lot of grant money and the like. Although she was sure the government wasn't expecting to pay for eyebrow shaping.

"How many weeks are we talking here?" With unlimited money and herself as a blank canvas, she might not see a free lunch hour until retirement.

"I'm putting you on the accelerated course," he informed her as he opened the glass door for her. "You should be finished within a month or six weeks."

Amy smiled at the news. She was doing better than she thought. Heh. Who would have thought?

"I don't know when this engagement party will take place," Marc continued. "But I'm using that event as your final exam."

Amy's smile froze. "Great." Just add another stress factor to the occasion. "Hey, we took a wrong turn. The art collection is on the main floor."

"We aren't looking at any art." He guided her down the steps to the basement. "It's time for your next class."

"Class? What kind of class?" He wouldn't sign her up for an art appreciation course.

"Dance class."

Her stomach twisted sharply. "Dance?"

"Yep." He stopped before a door. "Here we are. You'll be here on your lunch hours every Tuesday and Thursday. The teacher is allowing you to visit tonight as a personal favor. She has a waiting list from the women in the community for this particular class."

She took a step back. "I don't dance."

"That's why you're having the classes." He flashed a smile that made her tummy flip.

She refused to let him bedazzle her into dancing. "You don't understand," she said firmly. "I have no rhythm. Zip. Zero. Zilch."

"You'll be fine."

He didn't get it. She needed another tactic. "I don't have the right clothes. I haven't worn a tutu since I was three."

"No tutu or special shoes required." He moved to open the door.

"Really?" That was unusual. Most classes she'd taken in her youth required a complete wardrobe. "What kind of dancing is this?"

He swung open the door. "Bellydancing."

Her eyes widened. "No!" The metallic tang of panic filled her mouth.

"Stop stalling." He tried to wave her inside. "It's time for class to begin."

"I can't." She pressed her body against the cement wall next to the door. There was no way she was going to go shake her chest in front of strangers. Jiggle where she wasn't supposed to jiggle. No freaking way. "I'm not going to. You can't make me."

Marc's eyes narrowed at the challenge. He cornered her. Conflicting emotions crashed through her as she inhaled his warm, clean scent. She belatedly started her struggle as he slid his large hands behind her shoulders, prying her body off the wall.

"You can do this." Warning nipped his soft voice. "You will do this and everything else I throw your way. And do you know why?" he asked above the squeaking of her unyielding shoes. "Because you hate to fail."

The panic flashed brighter inside her. He knew what made her tick. Her muscles seized with surprise.

"I'm out of here." She dodged away from him, but Marc anticipated her move. Suddenly she was across the threshold watching the door close in her face.

"Have fun, Amy." Marc's voice wafted through the room as the door slammed shut. He stood in front of the door's window, bracing his feet slightly apart and folding his arms across his chest.

"Amy?" A woman in a sequined top and chiffon skirt was at her side. "Welcome to Bellydancing: Awakening the Goddess Within." She punctuated the greeting with the clink of finger chimes.

There was no escape, Amy realized as the teacher shook a diaphanous red scarf in her face. A shudder swept through her as the high wailing music pierced the air.

She glared at Marc through the window. He was going to pay dearly for this.

Chapter 3

Are you sexually aggressive?

Amy pressed her lips together as her pencil hovered over the "always" answer. A bead of sweat trailed down her spine. She ignored it, deciding it had nothing to do with guilt and everything to do with sitting in the institute's courtyard under the blazing sun.

She checked her watch again, wondering if it was time to meet Marc in his office. Amy growled when she realized she had plenty of time to complete the questionnaire.

A questionnaire worded in such a way that she already knew she'd failed.

This time the subjects revolved around color. She knew her color type: beige. She didn't need a survey to tell her that.

There was nothing wrong with beige. Nature had it. Why couldn't she? But according to Marc, studies showed that certain colors convey sexual messages. And from these questions, beige didn't even qualify.

Are you sexually aggressive? The question blared insistently at her like a neon light. If she chose "never," she would be stuck in the beige world forever.

If she lied and answered "always," she would get booted

up to red. But Marc would know she cheated again, which was so embarrassing because she was not a cheater.

It was essential now more than ever to tell the truth and to do her best. Not only because she needed quick results, but also because she needed to prove worthy of Marc's time and not have him regret sharing his expertise.

Amy looked down at her baggy white T-shirt and ankle-length khaki skirt. She sighed in defeat and reluctantly circled "never." Red made her look anemic anyway. Maybe Marc knew of a red-based beige.

"Amy? Is that you?"

No. The sarcasm burned on her tongue. She wished she could ignore the saccharine-sweet voice. But that would reveal too much.

"Hello, Tanya." Amy slowly raised her head, her lady-like smile already in place. It didn't falter as she noticed the other woman looking great in a flouncy red minidress and flirty shoes. Amy ignored the stab of envy and extended her hellos to Tanya's entourage.

The groupies consisted of several acquaintances from the library archives. They were the same women who last year had gossiped about Tanya over their morning coffee. It seemed that they really had been secretly worshipping her all the time. The women flanked Tanya like backup singers, probably hoping that her *Cosmo* look would rub off on them.

"You look different." Tanya eyed her critically. "Did you do something to your hair?"

"Took a pair of manicure scissors to it." Amy lied without compunction. She didn't want Tanya to know how hard she was trying to improve her appearance. The other woman would use that knowledge ruthlessly.

And there was no need for Tanya to know the lengthy involvement of her cutting her straight brown hair into a sexier, updated look. It was annoying that she could no longer pull her hair back into a ponytail, but Amy admitted that the layers accentuated instead of hid her face. Not that that was always a good thing.

Tanya arched her perfectly waxed eyebrows. "It looks . . . adorable."

Amy did her best not to glare. Adorable? If that wasn't a call for war. "Thank you. Are you guys getting off work?"

Tanya nodded, her blond hair glistening like gold in the hot sun. "We're heading over to look at the institute's ballroom. I'm reserving it."

"Ah." Amy paused. *And she's telling this to me because . . . ?*

"For my engagement party." Tanya used the words like well-aimed bullets.

Amy acted like the words missed their target. She pressed her hand against her cheek and widened her eyes. "That's right. I forgot about that."

"Oh, please tell me you'll be there. It wouldn't be the same without you."

Yeah, right. In what way? Did she need to flaunt her engaged status, or did she need Amy there so someone other than her backup group accepted the idea of everything being "just fine"? Or was Amy reading it wrong—was it all about having a big turnout?

"Let me know when it is."

"The fifteenth of next month."

"Okay." Amy nodded her head and wondered at the possibility of needing emergency surgery on that day. The chances were not good. "I'll have to check my calendar, but I'm sure I can be there."

Tanya turned around, ready to leave. "Oh." She snapped her fingers as she remembered something. "And you can bring a date."

Amy didn't particularly appreciate the snicker lurking under the invitation or the sly looks from Tanya's entourage. "I'll keep that in mind."

"If you like, I can set you up with someone."

"That won't be necessary." *Leave. Leave! I refuse to*

back off, but if you don't leave I'm going to say something that could give you the upper hand.

"If you're sure," Tanya said breezily. "It won't be any trouble."

Amy didn't want to know what kind of date Tanya would inflict on her. "I think I can handle that end on my own."

The confidence in her voice gave Tanya pause. "Oh, is it someone I know?"

Like I would tell you. "Perhaps."

"All right." Tanya started her retreat now that she wasn't so sure she had the upper hand. "See you around."

"Bye." Amy maintained the smile until they turned the corner. She heard Tanya say something about dating imaginary friends. The other women laughed.

Just you wait, Tanya. Amy's mouth twisted as she crumpled the questionnaire in her fist. *Just you wait.*

Marc slid the DVD into the player when his office door flew open. He looked up as Amy surged across the threshold. His heart stuttered at the vision.

Color bloomed in her pale face as her eyes glittered with energy. The white shirt and beige skirt drew tight against her slender frame, outlining every soft curve and gentle swell as she kicked the door shut.

He tore his gaze from the voluptuous lines he had always suspected were there. "You're late." His voice came out gruff, but Amy didn't seem to notice.

She approached him swiftly. Everything about her, from her swirling brown hair to her angry footsteps crackled with urgency. "Will you go out with me?"

Marc's breath blocked his throat as the world tilted. He cautiously straightened to his full height, wondering if he was hallucinating. "Excuse me?"

Her eyes lasered in on him with a staggering intensity.

"Kevin and Tanya's engagement party will be on the fifteenth next month. Will you go with me?"

Marc was going to hate himself for not prolonging the fantasy, but he needed to know. "Why?"

She tossed her dingy white tote bag onto the settee and paced the small room with choppy steps. "Tanya implied that I can't get a date."

He felt dazed. He still couldn't get over the fact that Amy asked him out. Or that he hadn't dropped to his knees in gratitude. "Can you?"

She whipped around, her loose hair fanning around her face. "Yes!" she hissed, offended that he should even ask.

Marc resisted the urge to soothe her bristling sensibility. Refrained from curling his fingers against her soft hair and brushing it out of her sparkling eyes. "Then why does her opinion bother you?"

Amy crossed her arms. "She said it in front of a small audience."

"Oh." Marc was beginning to realize Tanya was no dumb blonde. She knew how to hit and where.

"Just because I'm not a supermodel doesn't mean I can't get a date." Amy waved her finger in the air. "She's trying to intimidate me. Trying to make me act like a fool so she looks good."

Marc's eyes narrowed as he tried to comprehend what was going on. "You got all that by her questioning your dating ability?"

"You don't understand. She also made fun of my hair." She grabbed the ends between her fingers.

Okay, now he was lost. "Why? It looks good." Better than good. He wanted to tangle his fingers and sink into the warm softness, explore every inch before unraveling it at a leisurely pace from his satiny imprisonment.

"Oh." Amy's eyes shuttered and her anger dissolved. "Thanks."

"Amy, I'm taking you to the engagement party as your date." He made that clear before she started looking for an alternative escort. "So stop getting weird about it and focus your energy on this project."

"You'll go?" Her smile was brilliant but fleeting. "But what if I mess up your research?" She let out a horrified gasp. "What if I regress? What if I—"

Marc closed the distance between them. He silenced her by pressing his finger against her lips. He always imagined them to be soft, but the silkiness was a surprise. His hand tingled with heat as her bottom lip cushioned his fingertip. "I will take you no matter what and be proud having you at my side."

Amy's expression froze. She looked like she was at a loss for words as her mouth drifted open. His finger dragged down, catching the moist inner lip.

Marc wanted to rub his finger against her and dip it inside her mouth. He hesitated, fighting for control. Fighting for the power to step back.

He needed to step away immediately. He'd already said too much. It didn't matter that he wanted those words out in the open, that he felt no shame or insecurity from it. His only mistake was saying it too soon for her to luxuriate in the words.

Remembering that gave Marc the self-control he needed, and he slowly withdrew his hand. But he wouldn't consider taking back his words or diminishing them. He had said what he felt.

He turned, breaking the tension that was shimmering between them. "Let's get started."

"Fine, as long as it's not another multiple choice questionnaire." Her soft voice sounded shaky to him.

"It's not." He grabbed the DVD case off of the TV. "You're watching a movie."

"Whoa!" Her reaction startled him. She held her hands

up as if the box might be contaminated. "What kind of movie?"

His eyebrows soared. "What kind do you think?"

Amy was already backing away. "Okay, we may have a problem. I don't think I've ever seen anything X-rated."

"Then you should have no problem watching this." He shoved the case into her hands.

"*The Last Emperor*?" She scrunched up her face and handed it back. "You know what? Maybe now *would* be a good time to introduce me to soft porn."

Marc pushed it back into her hands. "This movie is a visual feast. And that's all I want you to do. Watch it, but with the sound off."

She looked incredulous. "For three hours?" Her voice raised an octave.

"Take notes. Whatever strikes you, write it down."

She turned toward the settee. "I could be home doing laundry," she muttered to herself.

"Or belly dancing."

She stopped in her tracks and slowly faced him. "What has my dancing teacher been telling you?"

"Nothing." Her reaction intrigued him. He leaned against the TV and crossed his ankles. "Is there anything I should know?"

"No." Her glare was arctic, indicating that the topic was closed. "Give me the remote."

Marc smiled and handed her the remote control. "Give me your questionnaires. You did do them, right? Answered them as Amy Bryce instead of Mae West?"

"Ha, ha, ha." Amy's eyes narrowed into slits and her jaw slid to the side. She marched over to the settee and rifled through her tote bag.

Deciding it might be a while before she found anything in that bag, Marc walked back to his desk. He sat down on his creaking chair as Amy approached him. She dropped crumpled paper, one wad at a time, on his cluttered desk.

He noticed how smears of pencil lead, eraser tracks and small rips marred the questionnaires. He looked up at her defiant face.

"Don't ask," Amy warned as she whirled back to her seat, "because you don't want to know."

Marc smoothed out the surveys and acted like he couldn't hear Amy's muttered predictions of being bored into a coma. As she plopped down onto the settee and started the movie, he felt the warm glow of accomplishment.

Not because of the questionnaires. A brief glance already warned him that the answers promised a lot of work. The scores would ultimately show a woman scared of her own sensuality, of her own feminine power.

The whirring electronic sound captured his attention. He glanced up at the TV and saw the scene going forward at warp speed. Marc slanted a warning look at Amy.

She flashed him a big, toothy, guilty smile. "Fast forwarding through the titles," she explained, hitting the play button.

"Uh-huh." The edge of his mouth quirked. Her mischievous attitude was his achievement. It was a definite improvement that she didn't feel the need to behave perfectly—that she would be comfortable enough to lower her guard, muttering her opinions. That she would rant about Tanya with the full knowledge that Marc wouldn't judge or hurt her because of it.

Get to work, Javier. He couldn't afford the time to moon over Amy. Because of his research project, he barely had time for this tutoring session. If he wanted to play it safe and smart, he would give Amy a stack of movies, a to-do list and send her on her way. But his wants were guiding him through this intimate project, which he knew was risky. Still, it didn't stop him from encouraging one-on-one lessons.

Marc shook his head in self-disgust and slowly made his way through the questionnaires. As he compiled the numbers, he frowned with concern. The scores were as low as he expected. The frown deepened as he heard the mechanical whir again. Marc decided to ignore it.

If only he could ignore Amy's presence. He fought the need to glance at her. It only made the rasp of her shirt on skin sound louder. The scratch of her pencil on paper took precedence to the numbers in front of him. Her tired sigh sounded like a whisper next to his ear.

Marc stared at the numbers in front of him, but they didn't make sense. He squeezed his eyes shut, determined to concentrate. Propping his elbow on the desk and cupping his forehead with his hand, he blocked his view of Amy.

Slowly, through the interspersing sound of pencils and fast forwarding, the numbers started to make sense. His skin tingled with awareness as he completed scoring the surveys in twice the time it should have taken.

As he wrote down a short reading list and the take-home assignment, he felt a shift in the atmosphere. The gradual tension wrapped around the small room.

Marc's pen slowed down as he heard the change in Amy's breathing. The tired sighs shortened. Held.

Against his better judgment, Marc darted a quick glance at her. Amy was enthralled. She held her pencil midway to her notebook. Heightened color suffused her cheeks. Her lips parted as she stared at the TV with slumberous eyes.

Marc glanced at the TV. *Oh . . . yeah*. The main character was in bed with his two wives. Pink-gold sheets cascaded over the three bodies, leaving the rhythmic movements up to the viewer's imagination.

The silky sheets didn't hide everything. The outline of hands was noticeable. Those exploratory hands stroked the bodies on both sides, inciting an urge from the voyeur to flip off the covers to see who was stroking whom.

The lighting cast a warmer glow on the sheets as it

formed into a billowing tent. The silky ripples quickly became frenetic waves.

Marc tore his gaze from the TV and swallowed hard. Images of Amy and him swathed in pink-gold flickered through his mind. His cock stirred as he decided the two of them could cause the sheets to stretch and tear.

But a threesome? No. No way. He wanted Amy exclusively. He didn't want anybody else. And when he did get Amy in his bed, he wasn't sharing. Ever.

The question was whether Amy would feel the same way. Did the scene grab her attention because of the sensual imagery? Or was she intrigued by the idea of three people in a bed?

As much as he wanted Amy, as much as he desired to have her in his bed, he could never agree to a threesome. Even if it was the only way he could have Amy. It would destroy his soul.

Marc stared blindly at the paper in front of him when he heard the buzz of the DVD player. His chest relaxed. Maybe he was wrong about what Amy found so fascinating. Maybe she wasn't ready for that in a movie, much less participating in the scenario.

He wondered what kind of scene she would consider safer. Marc looked at the TV and nearly choked when he saw the pink-gold sheets.

His mind couldn't wrap around the idea that she hit Rewind. That she needed to see the scene again. That maybe, just maybe, she found threesomes intriguing.

He cast a glance at her again, but he turned his head too sharply. The movement tore her attention away from the screen.

When Amy's eyes met his, the tension in the room clashed. The vibrations rippled through him. His soft shirt scraped against his sensitized skin and his erection was painfully constricted within his jeans.

Amy dragged her gaze away. Her tongue swept across her lips. She hesitated and opened her mouth to speak.

A loud knock on the door blistered the silence. Whatever Amy had to say was lost in the muffled shriek. She fumbled for the remote, pressing buttons randomly to turn off the movie.

Marc's heart pounded from the unexpected interruption. He tried to appear casual. "Come in."

Kayla swung open the door just as the TV screen went black. "Hey, Dr. Javier. Oh, sorry!" She started backing out as she saw Amy.

"That's okay, Kayla." He waved her inside. It was better this way, he decided. It would be smart not to act on the attraction between Amy and him. At least not now. "What's up?"

"I wanted to go over some of the data we've got so far for Reclaiming Your Sensuality," she said as she walked into the room and stopped in front of his desk. "It's not making sense, so I thought I should run it by you."

From the corner of his eye, Marc sensed Amy straighten in her seat as she heard the project mentioned. He slid a quick glance and saw the expectant expression. Why was she doing that?

His heart skipped a beat as it suddenly occurred to him. Amy still thought she was a part of the research. In such a case, she would be introduced to Kayla. All of his warning instincts went into full alert. What was he saying? Amy would be working exclusively with the research assistant.

He had to get Kayla out of the room before Amy put the introduction upon herself. And if Kayla discovered that he was conducting unauthorized sensuality tests on unsuspecting women, if his boss heard a hint of a rumor, it would be nothing short of disaster.

"I'll be down there in five minutes."

"Okay. Oh, are those more questionnaires? I don't

know how they got here." She reached for Amy's crumpled papers.

"No!" He lunged and scooped them up with one hand, startling both Amy and Kayla. "Uh, I mean, no, I haven't finished looking over these."

Kayla frowned. "But I—"

"I'll be there in five minutes," he repeated as he tapped the ends of the paper against the desk. "Promise."

"All right," Kayla agreed slowly as she backed out of the room. "Five minutes." She gave Marc another questioning look before nodding to Amy and departing.

When the door closed, Amy stood up. "I should get going, too." She reached for her tote bag. "Maybe I should watch the movie at home."

"Sure." Marc knew it was the right choice for Amy, but it didn't stop the disappointment welling up inside him. He wanted more time with her. "And you can take this reading list and your take-home assignment."

"Hey!" Amy's face clearly showed her displeasure. "You didn't say anything about homework." She clicked the DVD into its case and stuffed it into her tote.

"At the time, I didn't know I had six weeks to do this project."

"That's not my fault." She made a face and grabbed the paper from him. "All right, all right. What kind of homework are we talking here? Workboo—oh, my God!" She slapped her hand over her mouth.

Marc leaned forward in his chair, ready to grab her in case she fell. "Are you okay?"

"No, I am not okay!" She looked at the paper again as if she hoped she misread it. She turned paler instead. "This is outrageous."

He didn't expect her to take it that badly. He was going to have to finesse her into his way of thinking. "Now, Amy . . ."

"Don't you now Amy me. I can understand reading

these books and watching these movies." She jabbed her finger against the paper. "I can even go so far as to understand about visiting these Web sites. But . . . but . . ."

"Go ahead, Amy. You can say the word."

She waved the paper until it snapped in the air. "You want me to masturbate!"

Chapter 4

"You can't tell me to . . . do that." Her voice trailed off. She groaned inwardly. *Oh, yeah. That's telling him.*

Marc frowned. "Why not?"

Amy's jaw dropped. Was he serious? "It's . . . it's . . ." She didn't know where to start. "Private."

"Why?"

"Why?" she spluttered. "It just is! What makes you think you can just ask me? What are you going to do?" Her stomach flipped as one possibility occurred to her. "Grade me? Give me a 9.9 for artistic interpretation?"

"Being aware of your body is an important part of the process," Marc explained as he got up from his chair and walked around the desk. "You have to know how to give yourself pleasure."

Amy was already having enough trouble with the conversation when there was a desk between them. "Okay, that's enough." She raised her hands as if warding him off. "Really. Truly. Quite enough."

Marc continued to approach her. She dropped her hands before her fingers brushed against his chest. He stopped right in front of her and she had to tilt her head back to look at his face. His body heat wrapped around her. She felt cornered. Trapped.

"Amy," he asked gently, "how often do you masturbate?"

She gasped at the directness of his question. Even to her ears it sounded more like she was hacking up a hair ball. "What?!"

He gave her a look that seemed to cut through all the roadblocks she was throwing at him. "You heard me."

"Yeah, I heard you. I just can't get over the fact that you're asking me." Her eyes stung from bugging out.

"Get over it and stop stalling. What's your answer?"

"I'm not answering." She folded her arms across her chest. This project was getting way more personal than she had intended. She was all for the spa treatment, but she didn't want anyone to know what turned her on. Especially Marc, who already knew what made her tick.

"Once a week?" Marc asked. "Once a day? An hour?"

"None of the above," she answered tightly. She was trying so hard not to lie and randomly choose any answer he threw at her. She promised she wouldn't cheat, but he was making it very difficult.

"A month?"

"Would you stop?" Her face burned from blushing. Her teeth ached from clenching.

He tilted his head to the side and studied her face, "You do masturbate, don't you?"

Damn it! Amy wanted to stomp her foot. Why did he have to be so direct? Why couldn't he have dropped the subject that obviously made her uncomfortable?

"Amy?"

Her gaze darted all around the room. "Uh . . . I've been meaning to—huh,"—she pointed at the ceiling—"you have a spider web up in that corner—but I've been busy."

"God." He let out a weary sigh and dragged his hands through his hair. "I don't believe this."

"It's not a big deal. Just get a broom and swat at it."

He flashed a less-than-amused look. "I'm adding some

books to your reading list about masturbation. You should put the newfound knowledge to use. Immediately."

"Now?!" She didn't know if uteruses could shrivel in protest, but she was pretty sure hers just did.

"Not at this very moment," he said as he walked to one of his bookshelves. "Not with an audience."

The words "not yet" hung in the air, but she knew it was her imagination talking. "I am not going to masturbate on command. I won't do this and have you know I'm doing this."

"Why not?" He shrugged as he pulled out brightly colored books with bawdy titles she could never read while traveling on public transportation. "It's natural. It's healthy."

"Oh, right." She smacked her palm against her forehead. "That explains why it was recommended by a former surgeon general."

"It's important to the project," he answered as he walked back to her with a stack of books. "And to your own sensuality."

"Okay, fine." She grabbed the books before he got any closer. She clutched the books to her chest, effectively hiding the titles. "I just have to do it. Call it extra credit. Sure. No problem." She hurried toward the door while shoving the books in her tote.

"And," he called after her, "we'll discuss any questions you might have at our next tutorial."

Amy tensed and her fingers fumbled over one of the books. "Like hell we will." She quickened her step.

"We will," Marc countered as he followed her in a more leisurely stroll. "You can bet on it."

"Hey!" She whirled around and glared at Marc. "No one demands details about your last session."

"No one asked me before." His brown eyes took on an unholy gleam. "Are you asking?"

"Uh . . . I . . ." A renegade image clouded her vision. Of Marc naked. Steam curling around him as he stood in the shower. Rivulets of water trailing down his wet, bronze skin. His head thrown back, eyes squeezed shut, jaw clenched. The tendons of his neck bulging just under the skin.

"What do you want to know about it?" Marc asked. He placed his hands on his hips.

The voice and daydream intertwined. Amy swallowed as the image dipped past his naked waist. Her body tingled at the imagined sight of his large hands clasping his thick penis.

She could tell that it was heavy, hot and throbbing. He stroked himself hard. Fast. Each move crackled with power and need.

"Amy?"

She jerked at the sound of her name. She blinked and realized she was staring at his jeans. Ohmigod. She was checking him out and not being the least bit discreet about it. Amy hesitantly glanced up at his face. Marc's eyes were questioning, not glazed with lust. He was nowhere near aroused. Unlike her.

The heat from her blush sizzled the air. "I have to go." Her voice squeaked out and she twisted the reluctant doorknob.

"Do your assignment," he said as he opened the door for her.

She wasn't promising anything. "Maybe I will, maybe I won't."

"You better study hard, or our next tutorial will be hands-on," Marc said as he shut the door on her surprised expression.

Amy couldn't move a muscle if she tried. Her nipples beaded tight and her hands held onto her tote for dear life. But damn if his suggestion didn't unfurl her uterus like a parachute.

"Amy?" She heard the familiar voice over the festival games and rides. Turning around, Amy immediately spot-

ted Marc in the crowd. Her pulse soared with the sur-
rounding bells and whistles when her gaze connected with
his.

He was like a wild animal in a garden of delicate flowers. There was something primitive and earthy about him.
He looked out of place among the balloons and stuffed
animals displayed behind him.

Amy ignored the kick of desire flooding her bloodstream.
"Hey, Marc!" She waved him over to the cotton candy
stand. "About time you got here. I'm starving."

He strode toward her, every sure movement pulling at
his dark blue T-shirt and jeans, emphasizing the lean, mus-
cular lines of his body. "What are you wearing?"

She blinked and looked down at her voluminous green
cotton dress. "What I always wear . . ." Was this another
one of his trick questions?

"Where are the clothes we bought this week?" he asked,
his hands splayed out at his sides.

"You didn't say anything in the e-mail about wearing
them." She smiled her thanks at the vendor and accepted
the pink twist of spun sugar.

"I'm supposed to tell you these things? You have new
clothes. What woman wouldn't wear new clothes right
away?"

"I will after the makeover," she promised as she stepped
out of the line. She couldn't tell Marc that she wasn't ready
to wear them. She loved the outfits. They represented the
woman she wanted to be. They were bold and feminine.
Sexy. But she couldn't carry them off yet. Not until she
was the new, improved Amy. "They're after clothes, not
during," she explained.

Marc looked at her as if she spoke a different language.
"Says who?"

Amy shrugged off the question and tore off a piece of
the candy. "It's no big deal. I'm not here to give a fashion
show. According to your e-mail, I'm on a field trip to ex-

plore the sense of taste," she reminded, and popped the pink confection into her mouth. She closed her eyes as the sugar dissolved on her tongue. "Mmm. It's the best idea you've had yet."

"Is that right?" he asked gruffly.

Amy opened her eyes and saw Marc watching her intently. Her skin tightened as heat flushed through her body. Every feminine instinct that had lain dormant inside her was jarred awake.

What was wrong with her? Her wishful thinking was going to get her into trouble. She cleared her throat. "Would you like a piece?" she asked in a husky voice, and tore off another chunk before offering it to Marc. "It's kind of sticky."

Marc dipped his head and took the candy with his mouth. Amy's heartbeat stuttered as he never broke eye contact. His lips closed over her fingertips. She couldn't pull away from the moist heat. Didn't want to.

Her breath snagged in her throat when his tongue darted against her skin, sweeping away the sugar crystals. Her knees wobbled as she imagined his tongue sweeping against her pink core until she disintegrated in his mouth.

The festival colors twisted into a kaleidoscope. Her skin prickled under the summer heat. The music and laughter waffled in and out.

Marc grazed her fingers with the edge of his teeth. Amy yelped and jerked away. The topsy-turvy world set itself right with a thud.

"Tastes good," Marc said as he smacked his lips. "Can I have some more?"

She didn't trust the glitter in his eyes. Did he know she wanted to jump him and ride his tongue? Could he hear her heart pounding as she struggled to breathe?

"Uh. . . ." Her fingers flexed against the bag of cotton candy. She didn't realize she was still holding it, and shoved the candy between them like a shield. "Here."

The lingering traces of a country song clung in the air.

The fiddle plucked at her tense nerves, but she knew it was an excuse to escape. "Let's see what's going on there," she suggested.

Amy hustled to the edge of the makeshift dance floor, fully aware of Marc walking leisurely behind her. She needed to pull herself together before she did something stupid. Like rip off his clothes and make wild jungle love on the sidewalk.

The idea was sounding better with every second, and that's when she knew she was in trouble. Amy flinched when she felt Marc standing behind her. Her pulse skittered around like a game of marbles.

Amy tried to ignore the heat shimmering off of Marc's body and listened to the live band as the men and women swirled in front of her, dancing the two-step.

A strange longing filled her. She shifted uncomfortably as the need was right there, pushing underneath her skin. She tapped her toes to the beat, the movement tempering the pressure that spiraled tighter and tighter inside.

"Would you like to dance?" he asked, his mouth right above her ear.

She was surprised at how much she wanted to say yes. Wanted the music to invade her and take over. Have the song and Marc guide her. She craved to touch him under the guise of a dance.

"No, thanks," she declined reluctantly. Touching Marc would be like playing chicken with an oncoming train. "They haven't taught me the two-step in my bellydancing class." A class she kept skipping, but he didn't need to know that. "You go on ahead."

"That's okay." He reached around her and tore off another clump of cotton candy and ate it. She silently watched as he placed his thumb pad between his teeth and gently sucked off the sticky treat.

Amy pressed her thighs together as her clit swelled. She swerved her head and stared at the dancers who were now a blur. "I don't mind if you dance with someone else," she said in a rush. "Really. I'm not the jealous sort." At least, she didn't think she would be.

"I'm glad to hear it." His voice held a bite.

She shot him a questioning look. "Had problems with possessive girlfriends?" she hazarded a guess.

"No. I always remove myself from any situation that encourages jealousy before it can happen."

"Wow." Amy considered what he said as the band started playing a slow song. Marc had way more self-control than she could dream of. "I don't think I could do that."

"Yes, you could," he replied with absolute certainty. "You showed grace under fire this year. You thought before you acted."

She gave an inelegant snort. "A lot of good that did me." All that thinking made her look like a fool.

"You didn't get caught up in the drama. You showed class. Loyalty." His eyes shone with satisfaction. "I admire you all the more for it."

"Thanks." She stuffed her mouth with cotton candy, wishing it was a strap of leather she could chew. He admired her. Fantastic. Any hope she might have had about jumping into bed with Marc just fizzled.

She should be pleased, but a guy didn't break out in a sweat with admiration. Why couldn't he be just a little bit interested in her?

A flash of red caught her eye. Her muscles stiffened as she saw Tanya and Kevin on the dance floor. It was like watching two fully clothed people having sex and slithering off each other.

The cotton candy in Amy's mouth turned to sawdust as she saw Tanya's outfit. She had never seen the office slut go country, and she would have been happy without the visual. Neither the scanty red halter top nor the denim Daisy Duke shorts could contain all of the curves.

Amy felt a stab of envy. Not because Tanya had the body

to wear an outfit like that or because the blonde had Kevin's full attention. She wanted Tanya's confidence. If she had an iota of the woman's poise, Marc would be panting with more than admiration.

But she wasn't going to strut her stuff anytime, anywhere soon. Thank God she hadn't tried to unveil her new look today. How could she convince everyone that she was better than ever without Kevin when they were going to compare her to Tanya? It was like comparing Mary Poppins to Madonna.

A wave of nausea slapped her as she realized her sensuality plan really was akin to Mission Impossible. "You know, I think I've had enough of this food," Amy murmured to Marc as she placed a hand on her stomach. "I should go home now."

They were in big trouble, Marc decided as he walked Amy along the tree-lined parking lot to her car. The festival was going on full tilt in the distance, but the music no longer tickled Amy's senses.

He had seen how she'd almost burst out of her cocoon. He foamed at the mouth with anticipation, waiting, watching, ready to see her take flight.

And then she had seen Tanya and Kevin.

Marc gnashed his teeth with frustration. The bastard didn't deserve Amy. Not her love, her attention or even the work she put into her transformation.

It was aggravating. He didn't want Amy to transform for Kevin. Hell, he hadn't wanted Amy to transform at all. He loved everything about her, her bad choice in men notwithstanding, and suffered many sleepless nights wondering if he was making a big mistake.

But he had underestimated the power of the woman lurking underneath Amy's public image. He was in awe and he wanted more than anything to watch her break out before she could achieve her full glory.

It was a unique brand of hell to create the woman of his dreams he had no right dreaming about. A woman he loved too much to fail. A woman he was going to lose when his creation proved successful. Lose to Kevin.

The bilious green rope of jealousy wrapped around his chest. What a liar he was about removing himself from any situation that promoted jealousy. He was knee-deep in it.

He looked over at Amy and his heart squeezed. She was deep in thought, her brow furrowing. He wanted to smooth the lines away with a caress. A kiss. Not that she would notice. She didn't seem to realize he was there.

He cleared his throat and saw Amy start at the sound. "How's the reading assignment going?" he asked.

She made a face. "Ugh."

"And the masturbation?"

"Sheesh! Marc!" Amy was a blur of motion. His back collided against the trunk of a tree. Amy's hand clapped over his mouth. "Do you mind?" she said in a hissing whisper, and looked around to see if anyone had heard.

"Sorry." Her hand muffled his voice. "But how is it going?"

She glared at him. "Great," she answered brightly and pulled her hand away from him.

Marc straightened away from the tree. "It is?" Suspicion clouded inside his mind. That didn't sound right, unless she had discovered the perfect masturbation muse. He didn't want to know who it was. He truly didn't want to know that it was Kevin. "How often are you doing it?"

"Enough that I thought I was going blind," Amy admitted as she stepped back onto the sidewalk. "Turned out to be a false alarm."

Marc felt his eyebrows rise as he watched her move briskly down the sidewalk. It looked like she was trying to get away. "I don't believe you."

"The earth moved," she said without a backward glance. "Angels wept. I saw a bright light at the end of the tunnel."

"Amy," he warned.

She halted abruptly. "Okay!" She stomped her foot and turned to face him. "I'm trying. I really am."

"Trying?" After all this time, she was still *trying*? If only he could guide her through masturbation. Step by step with lots of repetition until she was addicted to his touch. But had that been the case, she would have learned nothing and he would be suffering from carpal tunnel syndrome. "That's it." He strode to her and pointed his finger in her face. "You are on probation."

She huffed with disbelief. "I don't think so! I have never been on academic probation and I'm not about to start now!"

"You don't get it." Marc rubbed the back of his neck as he decided on his next move. He had wanted to keep this from her because her confidence already took too many hits. Obviously, he had made the wrong choice. "You're failing."

"I'm—?" Her voice drifted to silence and she looked away. "How badly?"

Marc cupped her shoulder with his hand. He didn't know how to say it gently and get the message across. "You should be in the intermediate steps, but you're still in the formative stage." He felt her tense from his words and he silently called himself every name in the book.

"With only four more weeks to go." She nodded her head with short, choppy moves. "Okay." Amy stepped away from him and pressed the key ring button to unlock her car.

He bunched his fingers together and let his hand drop to his side. "Don't worry about the time. Focus on your studies. It's time to apply yourself."

"Yeah." She got into her car with automatic moves, her face void of any expression. "Yeah, sure."

"Are you okay?" He would hate himself forever if he destroyed her confidence.

"Of course." She looked up at him and flashed him a distant, polite smile that cut him deeper than any sharp words. "Thanks for the progress report."

He grabbed the top of the car door before she could shut it. "For what it's worth, I believe in you. I know you can be whatever you want to be."

Amy's eyes glistened with unshed tears. "Really?"

"Yeah, really." God, he wanted to kiss her. And not the comforting kind, either. A deep-throat, devouring kiss. But that would be bad timing. And once he kissed her, he wouldn't stop. He would be rutting her against the dashboard in a minute flat.

With great reluctance, he stepped back. "But it's not going to be easy," he continued, wishing his voice didn't sound so rough. "We have a lot to do for your midterm exam next week."

Her groan soothed his raging blood. Now if only he could maintain the teacher mindset for four more weeks. It didn't look good.

She was failing! Amy stared at the ceiling in the pitch-black room, unable to sleep although the clock at her bedside said it was after midnight. Her! Amy Bryce, *aka* The Brain, was failing in a class. An independent study, at that! It was unheard of.

But then, she had never been graded on her sensuality quota. Amy screwed her eyes shut, desperately trying to ward off the truth. She wasn't sensual and never would be.

She couldn't fail. Amy opened her eyes and exhaled. Not in front of everyone at that stupid engagement party. Definitely not in front of Marc.

Marc. Amy suddenly couldn't lie still. She twisted and arched, the bedsheets tangling around her legs. She wished she had accepted his offer to dance. She wished a lot of things about Marc. Impossible things.

Okay. Enough stalling. If she wasn't going to be sensual, she would at least fall back on doing what she did best. Be the perfect student. If she wasn't going to wow the teacher with her aptitude, she would dazzle him with perfect attendance, beautiful penmanship and most improved progress. Amy laced her fingers and cracked her knuckles. It was now or never.

She dipped her hand under the cotton sheets, flipped back her nightshirt and cupped her sex. Okay . . . she felt stupid. She wasn't wet. Not even aroused. She should have first found out how much extra credit was involved with masturbation.

Be patient, she warned herself as she slid her fingers along her flesh. *Think of something else. You have to organize the Delta Delta Alpha reunion. Buy that birthday present for Jennifer. Finish the homework assignment.*

Why was she even doing this? she wondered with every short, halfhearted rub. She had had good sex without self-pleasuring. Kevin had given her orgasms without having to "prepare" her. She wasn't sure if her ex even knew she had a clitoris. Marc would know. Not only that, but he would know what to do with it.

The vision billowed in her mind before she could stop it. She easily imagined Marc naked and kneeling between her legs. Slick with sweat and focused only on pleasuring her. He had one hand teasing her nipple, his other hand pressing against the damp folds between her thighs.

Amy gasped as her clitoris swelled. A warm, syrupy sensation invaded her, weighing down her pelvis. She arched her back and bore down with her hips, trying to alleviate the sudden pressure.

Huh. The pressure wasn't necessarily uncomfortable. She wiggled her waist as the sensations seeped through her abdomen. It actually felt . . . good.

Her other hand inched to her breast and she fondled it the way she dreamed Marc did while her other fingers stroked her glistening slit. She closed her eyes, the image of Marc strong and clear. Amy felt breathless, wondering what he would do to her next.

His long, lean fingers dipped into her core. The back of Amy's knees tingled and she parted her legs more. Goose bumps swept across her skin as he teased her nipple, drawing circles—smaller and smaller—to the tip.

Amy's heart thudded in her ears as Marc teased her with his hands. She rocked from side to side as the anticipation built inside her. She didn't know how high it would build, or how far she would fall.

She squeezed her eyes as she imagined Marc pleasuring her. He was as aroused as she. His skin was drawn tight against his features, his eyes dark and glittery, his cock slapping against his stomach, desperate to bury deep and snug into her wet heat.

And then he pinched her nipple hard as he pressed her swollen clit between his fingers. A swift and thunderous orgasm rolled through her. She dug her heels into her mattress and let out a keening cry as the jagged climax ripped through her mind and soul.

Amy collapsed against the crumpled sheets. She gulped for air as her legs and arms shook. Opening her eyes, she blinked back the bright spots and stared at the dark ceiling.

Whoa. Her brain slowly pieced itself back together like a jigsaw puzzle. Her first fragmented thought was that

Kevin had a lot to answer for. She also wondered how it would feel if Marc sucked her clit.

She felt her tired lips slant into a wicked smile as she nestled her hand against her puffy, wet core that throbbed to the beat of her heart. Well, there was a sure way to find out. . . .

Chapter 5

The extra credit was really working for her, Marc decided. He didn't ask if she was doing it. He didn't need to. He saw it in the way she walked, the way she stood. Even the way she brushed her hair away from her eyes said it all. She was aware of her body and took pleasure from it.

Damn.

He wanted to take pleasure from her body, too. The lusty greed threatened to explode through his skin. He wanted to *give* her pleasure as well. Show her how he felt with every touch. Kiss . . . Taste . . .

Marc looked down at the table and slowly unclenched the handle of his beer mug. As he watched the color bleed back into his whitened knuckles, Marc wondered how Amy always had the ability to surprise him. He thought he knew her. Understood her.

And then she managed to shock the hell out of him.

Like this midterm exam. He told her he would pretend to be her date and asked her to choose a place she felt most comfortable. A place where she could unveil her new look in front of people she knew.

For some reason, he expected they would play it safe and go to a restaurant. Maybe do Trivia Night with her friends from the institute's library. Sitting next to her at the seedy neighborhood bar was something of a surprise.

He didn't know what she saw in the decrepit building and the hodgepodge of people sitting in mismatched tables and chairs. He had to admit that the rock band, which consisted of some people he saw behind the meat counter at the grocery store, was really good. But he couldn't imagine Amy was there for head-banging music.

The people obviously knew her. They said "hey" and gave her a wine cooler without her asking. They did lots of double takes at her new, improved appearance.

Only Marc wasn't too sure about that improved part. He didn't think there was anything wrong about the way Amy used to be. He wouldn't even say it was a better transformation. Just different.

"Marc?" Amy's voice wafted over him. "Marc?"

He braced himself. "Yeah?" He turned and silently congratulated his preparation. If he hadn't, he would have pounced on her.

What Amy wore was not all that different from that of the people at the bar. But it was a milestone to her and it was also a reason for him to beg for mercy. Her jeans fit snugly against her lush ass. The chunky belt dipped low enough to offer glimpses of her navel and silky skin. Her T-shirt sported a trendy logo, but it was hieroglyphics to him. He only noticed her firm breasts thrust proudly against the thin cotton.

It was more than how she looked that got him in the gut and in the groin. Sure, she smelled so good that he wanted to nuzzle her neck and find where the scent originated, but it was her attitude that knocked him off his feet. He was spellbound by the mischievous sparkle in her eye, the bring-it-on body language, the—

"Never mind," Amy said with a smile that made him want to chew off the lip gloss from her mouth. She turned her attention back to her friend Nicole before he could lunge.

He guzzled the last dregs of his beer and noticed yet another regular giving him the once-over. Nice to see that people were protective of her, but it bristled against him. Why were they worried about him? And what was wrong with their radar when Kevin was around?

He wanted them to know that he was nothing like Kevin. He wasn't even a real date. More like . . . hell, he wasn't quite sure what he was.

Marc expelled a deep sigh. Yes, he did. He was here as her tutor and he had to give her a midterm exam. As thrilled as he was at her progress, he sensed it was skin-deep. If he wanted her to achieve her goal, he had to challenge her confidence.

He knew of one way to test her. Marc turned to Amy. "Do you want to dance?" he asked, and tilted his head in the direction of the dance floor.

Amy hesitated. "Is that part of the exam?"

"Absolutely." Both her confidence and his self-control were going to be put to the test.

She scrunched up her nose. "Then I decline."

Yep, she would take an incomplete rather than risk a failing grade. "Aw, Amy," Marc said with a teasing lilt. "I think you're chicken."

"Bwak, bwak."

"What's there to be scared of?"

Amy flashed him a look. Her guard wavered. For one infinitesimal moment, he caught a glimpse of what she always tried to hide. Amy blinked and looked flustered before she hurriedly turned away and launched into a conversation with Nicole.

Marc stared at her, shaken. He saw deep into her soul. It was exhilarating. Terrifying. He felt the knowledge zooming at him before taking a direct hit.

All of a sudden, he knew. He understood, and the knowledge pierced clean through him. It was more than the fear of being seen. It was of being noticed and then discounted. It was easier, less painful, to be invisible.

"Dance?" a smoky voice above his head asked.

Marc glanced up and saw a bodacious blonde standing next to him, her gaze traveling up and down his body. Poured into a denim miniskirt and halter top, the woman showed off her assets with weary indifference. Marc wasn't interested in the woman or the dance. He wanted Amy even if she took to wearing ugly muumuus and converted to a religion that forbade music.

He was about to refuse and make it known that he was with Amy when he realized this was the challenge he'd been looking for. Or was it? His heart pounded with indecision. He didn't want to slight Amy or hurt her feelings, but would he back away from this kind of test for his other test subjects?

The answer clanged through his head immediately. No. He would go full steam ahead once he determined it wouldn't cause irrevocable damage. If he knew it would do them good, Marc wouldn't care if the participants hated him for the rest of their lives.

But this wasn't about a test subject. This was about Amy. He didn't want to fall from grace. He didn't want to lose this chance with her. Lose her.

Marc turned to Amy and met her gaze head-on. This was the moment of truth. "I'll be right back," he said.

He felt his heart hesitate as Amy grew completely still. Would she fight this head-on challenge to her sexual allure or would she instantly give up?

"Sure," she said brightly as her glow evaporated. She looked past him and gave a ladylike smile. "Hey, Donna."

Disappointment crashed through Marc. She had given up without a fight. He rose from his seat and escorted the woman to the dance floor as dread ate away at him. He had taken a risk with Amy and had nothing to show for it.

Amy walked the few blocks back to her home with Marc at her side. She kept a casual pace as the buzzing streetlights guided her path. She answered Marc's occasional questions in an even tone. Her arms were down at her sides, her hands flat, fingers uncurled.

No one would guess that she wanted to wring his neck.

"That was a good band," Marc said.

At some time during the night, the music transmuted into a constant high-pitched buzz and contributed to her headache. "Uh-huh."

"Their final song rocked."

How did he notice, when the slut was all over him like a rash? And that woman knew all about rashes. She wasn't called VD Donna for nothing.

"I had a good time. What about you?"

"Yep." She did. Right up until he accepted another woman's offer to dance. While he was with *her*. Yes, she had declined his offer, but he'd had her dress up and be seen among her friends, only to embarrass her like that. Even Nicole was ready to kick him in the shins.

At least he hadn't spent the entire evening with VD Donna. Although Amy wasn't sure if that was a good thing. He'd danced with other women—wallflowers, good-time girls, you name it. Each time he said he'd be right back. Each time she smiled her consent and said nothing. It got harder to smile. It had been a struggle not to leave.

Amy didn't know why she was so upset. She understood why guys picked the slut over her. It was the way the world turned. But even if there were no sluts around, guys still didn't see her. She usually didn't care. This time it cut like a knife.

Marc's long-suffering sigh shattered her thoughts. "Okay, let me have it."

"Hmm?" she asked innocently.

His glance indicated he was not fooled. "You closed up the moment Donna came to our table."

She drew her head back and frowned. "I don't know what you're talking about."

"Yeah, you do." His expression made her drop her pretense. "You didn't expect me to take her up on her offer."

Was she that transparent? "Why did you?"

"Because I wanted to test your level of confidence. You never had a direct attack on your sexual allure."

"Oh, really?" Amy stopped and placed her hands on her hips. "What do you call all those quizzes I've been taking?"

"Those quizzes tested how much you retained the information." He pointed a finger at her. "Tonight you were supposed to apply it. Guess what? You didn't."

"I did too." No way was he going to tell her she had failed her midterm. "I could tell you everything about the five senses."

"The senses are the foundation of your sensual journey. You still need the confidence. How are you going to walk into Kevin and Tanya's engagement party and not get clobbered by a woman who would take you down?" He splayed his hands in the air. "And I'm talking verbally. Psychologically. Physically. She'd do it if you so much as sniff around her man."

Amy shot him a withering glare. Sniff around Kevin? For what? Did Marc really think she was that desperate, that pathetic, to want Kevin back? "You have no idea what you're talking about," she declared and marched on.

"Yeah, I do." He reached out and grabbed her upper arm. She instinctively pulled away, but she couldn't budge. "You want to go to this engagement party and make your mark, but you are clueless if you think Tanya won't fight for Kevin. And that is where she has the edge."

"Because she fights dirty?" Amy asked distractedly as she made an exaggerated production of trying to escape.

"She's not afraid to fight for her man," Marc clarified. "She's not afraid to go after what she wants. You are."

Amy froze. *Ouch*. Trust Marc to give it to her straight. Did he have to put it like that? Did he have to make Tanya sound more admirable than she?

"You make yourself invisible because you're afraid," Marc continued relentlessly. "Afraid of rejection."

She had to stop it before his words cut too deep. "That's not true." Amy hated how her voice wavered.

"You never fought for Kevin. Never made a public claim on him. And what happened? The minute Tanya set eyes on him, you looked the other way."

Her mouth dropped open. "Oh, so I'm to blame?" She tried to shake her arm out of his hold. "If Kevin loved me, he would have stayed with me."

Marc's eyes widened with surprise. "I'm not blaming you!" He dropped her arm and shoved his hands in his hair. "I'm saying that claiming your mate goes a long way."

Amy scoffed at the idea. "So says a man who detests jealousy."

Marc took a deep breath. She felt his frustration boiling under his skin. "Jealousy and possessiveness are different," he replied quietly. "What I'm trying to get across is that you refused to claim possession."

"Making it easier for people to steal from me," she finished for him and rolled her eyes. "Your point is duly noted. But remember this, if I had to claim possession to keep him, he wasn't that much of a keeper."

Marc nodded in agreement and suddenly swiveled his head. "What?" He waved his hands to stop. "Back up. Isn't this the same guy you want to get back?"

She wrinkled her nose. "Get Kevin back? Hell, no, why would I do that? I just managed to get rid of him."

Marc's eyes looked like they were going to bug out. "Then why—when—why . . ."

"Am I taking part in your project? Why am I trying to reclaim my sensuality?" She shrugged. "I'm tired of people pitying me."

The shocked look on Marc's face almost made her want to laugh. "Everyone at the party is going to know that I'm doing just fine," she announced, and strode down the sidewalk. "You'll see."

Marc stared after her. He couldn't move as thousands of emotions crashed inside him. After months of wanting and waiting, after weeks of keeping his distance and refraining from touching her, *now* she told him?

She didn't want Kevin. She didn't even like Kevin. She was free to pursue. She had been all this time.

He couldn't decide what to do. Kick himself? Howl at the moon? Pounce?

One thing was for sure, he was going to get Amy and make her his woman, his mate, his wife. Possess her completely. He had no problems making his claim.

And she'd know it, too, Marc decided as he walked to her, easily catching her with his brisk, purposeful strides. She'd know it whether he had to place a ring on her finger or tattoo his name on her ass.

"How are you going to prove that you're just fine?" Marc asked.

"I'm going to walk into the party with my head held high." Amy punctuated her statement with a swagger.

He swallowed roughly as he watched the sway of her hips. "That's it? You think that's going to work?" He dragged his gaze back to her profile. "How did that work for you in the bar?"

Amy's eyes narrowed from his pointed jab. "Marc, you

worked so hard and I appreciate it from the bottom of my heart, but we need to face the facts." She stopped at the steps to her apartment building and turned to face him. "I'm not a good match for this sensuality project. I think I should do us both a favor and quit."

Quit? The word hit him like a sucker punch. Damn, he should have seen that coming. Now that she had to dig deep and face her fears, she was ready to quit. He had to come up with something that would be more difficult to deal with. But what?

"Well, okay, Amy. If you feel that way. And I guess you should find yourself another date for the party."

"You're not— Never mind."

Going back on his word chafed at him. He had to believe the ploy would work. "I'm not going to stand by and watch you take on the world when you haven't been fully trained."

"Gee, how noble of you." Her eyes were narrowed into slits. "It's too late to find a date now. Thanks."

"I could change my mind, but that means you would have to finish the project."

She stomped her foot. "You said you would take me to the party no matter what." Anger flashed through her eyes.

"It's true. I did." He raised his hands in a hopeless gesture. "But you changed your mind and I have to change mine."

Her lips pressed together in a mulish line. "Fine. I'll finish the stupid project." With a huff she turned around and clomped up the stairs.

Relief poured through him. "Good," he said as he followed her to the door.

She whirled around to glare at him. "And you're taking me to the party. It *is* my final exam. Believe me." She pressed her finger into his chest. "I will be ready."

He looked down at her finger and raised an eyebrow. And then he knew what to do. He smiled as the plan rapidly formed in his mind. He wasn't going to pounce. He was going to be the prey.

"Glad to hear it," he said huskily, "but your exam is going to happen earlier." Just not fast enough for him.

Her jaw slid to the side in annoyance. "Stop messing with my mind, Marc. You need to give me some warning. Where are you taking me?"

"I'm not. You're taking me." He stepped onto the landing next to Amy. Raising his arm and placing his hand next to her head, he towered over her. "Your final exam is to seduce me."

She blinked and stumbled back, colliding with the door. "What?" she barely breathed out. Emotions chased each other across her face. Surprise. Intrigue. She settled for indignation. "I have never slept with my teacher for a grade and I'm not about to start now."

"I said seduce." He leaned in, inhaling her scent, watching the pulse in her neck flit like a caged butterfly. "Make me pant with need for you," he said gruffly. "Make me get on my knees and beg for you."

She gazed at him with wild eyes before swallowing visibly. "That's it?"

"That's it," he promised with his heart in his throat.

"Piece of cake." Her voice came out in a squeak and she cleared it nervously. "You're a guy, after all."

He was glad she noticed. "Then what have you been so afraid of?" he taunted as he dropped his hand.

She drew up to her full height. "I'm not afraid. And I will seduce you," she vowed with a glint in her eye.

"I'm looking forward to it." More than she would ever know. "Can't wait to see what your first move will be." He turned and hopped down the stairs. "Oh, and Amy?"

"What?" she asked in a waspish tone.

He stopped and looked over his shoulder. "I might be a guy, but that doesn't make me a sure thing." He flashed a smile. "Sweet dreams," he said and walked away before his luck ran out.

Chapter 6

He blew it.

His best opportunity to have Amy Bryce and he messed up royally. Marc strode to his office as the sun began to set, angry at himself as he had been for the past week.

This was what happened when he didn't follow the plan. When he got impatient and grabbed. When he acted on his feelings instead of his methods.

He couldn't even lose himself in his work. Reclaiming Your Sensuality was supposed to be his breakthrough research. Only he proved what an inefficient intimate communicator he could be. Now all he wanted was a breakthrough with Amy.

Instead of a breakthrough he had apparently broken things off with her. Her vow to seduce him was just words. Bravado. Bullshit.

She couldn't even face him. They played phone tag. His impromptu visits to the library resulted in "just missing" her. She responded to his e-mails with vague answers, leaving him frustrated. Hungry. Desperate for a glimpse of her.

He got the message loud and clear. He'd scared her off. Now he had to make amends and figure out how to win her back. It was going to be difficult since he never had her in the first place.

Standing by his office door, Marc searched for his keys. He paused when he heard a faint strain of music. It sounded like a sitar. From his office. That couldn't be right. He hadn't been in his office all day.

Marc unlocked the door and opened it a crack. The scent of sandalwood curled around him. He inhaled deeply at the incense. It beckoned him in and he pushed the door farther.

His office had been transformed. The lights were off and the shades were drawn. Strands of tiny white Christmas lights outlined the walls, casting a starlit glow to the room. Glittery ribbons in every color of the rainbow hung from the ceiling.

He shut the door and stepped forward, only to look down when his foot crushed the rose petals strewn across the floor.

"*Namaste*, Marc."

His head jerked up and his gaze clashed with Amy's. The sheaf of papers fell from his hand as he saw her standing in the middle of the room, shrouded in the shadows.

Amy wore a scarlet red silk sari. Her brown hair fell loosely against her shoulders. Her bare feet and dipped head suggested humility, but her kohl eyes advertised something else entirely.

Marc took an instinctive step back. "Amy." His voice sounded strangled. She moved forward. The tiny bells on her anklet jingled as her gold bangles clinked against each other.

He belatedly realized she held a brass tray filled with sweets. She dipped her vermillion-tipped nails in a shallow bowl and grasped a rock of sugar. She slid the sugar in his mouth before he could speak.

The sweetness exploded in his mouth. The musky incense clouded his mind. The rasp of silk and the chime of gold intensified in his ears.

Be strong. . . . He must not weaken.

"Please take off your shoes." Amy gave a gentle command.

Marc already toed off one sneaker when he realized he did as she suggested without question. "What is all this, Amy?" he asked as she placed the tray on his desk.

"Sssh." She pressed a finger on his lips. It was all he could do not to draw it in his mouth and suck fiercely. The image made his cock twitch.

"Won't you sit down?"

Oh, God. When did she learn the eye-batting move? "Only if you tell me why you avoided me for the past week."

"I was planning this night and I didn't want to ruin the surprise. I wasn't too sure about the sari. It keeps falling down." The silk slithered from her shoulders as she spoke.

Marc clenched his hands, fighting the need to grab the end of the sari and unwrap her. He had a clear vision of them naked and tangled in scarlet silk.

He winced as his cock pressed painfully against his jeans. He wasn't going to act on his impulses. Act on his fantasies. That would end the final exam. And, God help him, he wanted to know what she would do to seduce him.

"Marc?" she gestured at the settee.

"No," Marc said, and folded his arms across his chest. "I'm fine where I am."

Amy pressed her lips together, her heart pumping furiously. Didn't Marc understand how much courage it had taken to set herself up for this night? The research wasn't difficult—research was her life.

It took more courage than she had to make a great big fuss. He knew she made the effort and she couldn't blow it off. It took all the self-confidence she had to offer her body for his pleasure. Most of all, she was facing certain probability of rejection.

And she would get rejected—not because of her, but because of his teaching methods. She had to remember that as he made the night as challenging as possible. It was a good thing he didn't know she was fulfilling her fantasies under the guise of the final exam.

But the night looked like it was going to be shorter than she planned. Marc didn't fall for the whole sensual setting, Amy realized as she gnawed on her lip. He showed no signs of appreciating the Indian theme. She hadn't counted on that.

It was time to go to plan B: block the door.

"You dropped your papers," she said. They looked like statistical analysis, probably for his sensuality project. "Let me pick them up for you." She made a direct line for the exit, her gold anklets and bangles clinking madly.

"No!" Marc leaped forward. "That's—"

He grabbed her arm and Amy turned abruptly, slipping on the rose petals. She reeled back, snatching at the air as they fell onto the floor. "Ow!" she moaned as the crushed, fragrant petals fluttered around her feet.

"Why are you complaining?" Marc sat up, rubbing his arm. "I'm the one who broke your fall."

Amy didn't smile back. She couldn't believe the mess she had made out of this night. And she'd really thought it was going to work. "I guess we don't need to continue," she said calmly as defeat weighed down on her.

"Why?" He shook the feeling back into his hand. "Do you think tripping me is the same as me getting on my knees? I don't think so. And before you even try, knocking the air out of my lungs doesn't count as panting."

Amy glared at him. Well, if he wasn't willing to give up, neither would she. "Did you get hurt?"

He jerked back as if her touch might burn him. "I'm okay," Marc said warily.

She ignored his macho display and grabbed his wrist. Her pulse quickened as a thick awareness flared between them. "Let me see." She inspected his hand and kissed the reddened spot, noting how his skin tasted essentially *him*. "There. All better."

He didn't pull away. She felt his eyes boring into her. "You missed a spot."

"Where? Here?" She pressed her mouth next to her first kiss, surprised at the shower of sparks that invaded her blood. "Or here?" She darted her tongue on his skin.

Amy heard his sharp intake of breath. "All over."

Hiding a smile she was sure was as ancient as time, Amy lapped his hand with the tip of her tongue, making a path from his wrist to his palm. She found that his hands trembled more when she gave her attention to the skin between his fingers. She dawdled there, wanting to give him maximum pleasure.

Amy slowly made it to his fingers, licking and kissing until she got to his thumb. Covering her mouth over his thumb, she sucked it hard. Marc shuddered and moaned.

"Marc?" Her voice slurred around his thumb. "Are you panting?"

He cleared his throat with a rough cough. "No."

She released his hand. "Do you want me to kiss you, Marc?" She crawled over his legs, the scarlet silk dragging against his faded jeans. She quivered with her own need as the sari brushed against her sensitized skin. "Do you want me to lick you everywhere?" she asked as her lips almost touched his. "Kiss you all over?"

His body clenched underneath her. She saw the muscle in his jaw bunch. "Only if you mean it," he answered.

"You'll have to ask me nicely," she whispered as she placed a series of kisses along his taut jaw line. He tasted warm. Male. "You might have to . . . beg."

"If there's going to be any kissing done, it will be you who does the begging."

"I can't wait." She trailed her kisses toward his mouth,

the shadow of his beard scratching her lips. Marc dodged out of her way. Amy froze, startled.

"You don't need to continue, Amy," he said harshly. "You passed your final exam."

She recoiled as if she had been punched. Her arms and legs felt jittery. Amy stared openmouthed at Marc, but he appeared fascinated by the wall on the other side of the room.

"Oh." Tears burned behind her eyes. "That's . . ." The automatic cool reply died on her tongue. She couldn't do it. She couldn't hide behind the ladylike mask this time. She wanted him more. Wanted him more than she wanted to save face.

"Didn't I mention it?" She tried to sound casual, but her shaking voice spoiled the effect. "I decided not to take the exam."

Marc turned, ensnaring her with his eyes. "What? Why? No, *when* did you decide this?"

She leaned closer, her stomach jumping at the prospect of getting pushed away. "Marc," she said huskily as she licked his cheek to his ear, tasting the clean skin with the flat of her tongue, "if I didn't want to seduce you, I would have told you where to shove your challenge."

Amy could feel the restraint he held over his body. It made her hot, even though she craved his hands on her. She wanted to experience his brand of mastery directed at her. "But I want to seduce you," she continued, nibbling a long-forgotten piercing on his earlobe. "I want you."

Marc radiated with a building tension. She couldn't wait for his stubbornness to crumble. She felt wet and achy with anticipation.

"Tonight was for you, not for the grade." She'd never felt more courageous, more scared out of her mind. "I wanted to please you. Seduce your senses. Make you want me."

He closed his eyes, the stark need hardening his features. But he remained silent.

"Do you want me, Marc?" she asked. She couldn't ask more plainly, and her chest constricted anxiously. She timidly outlined his eyelid with the tip of her tongue. "Can I have you?" *Please say yes . . . please say yes . . .*

"Oh, God, yes." His voice rumbled.

Heat flooded through her at his words. She felt more than victorious. She felt powerful. Womanly. "I want to kiss you. I've been wanting to for so long."

When her mouth touched his, Marc shoved his hands into her hair and cradled the back of her head. He drew her closer and devoured her mouth.

She dove into him, tasted the curves and lines of his lips before darting her tongue inside his mouth. Sensations washed over her. Passion. Love. Need. Worship. She greedily accepted it all and gave back more.

Amy explored his mouth as Marc's hands caressed her body. She nipped with her teeth and licked the inside of his lips. Reveling in the sounds of his moans and fragmented whispers, she captured his tongue with her mouth and sucked.

"My turn," he growled. "I want to lick every inch of you."

Her knees wobbled at the blatantly masculine demand. She rose shakily to her feet. "Help me out of this sari."

He yanked the silk from her shoulder and gave a fierce tug. The pleats she so painstakingly created disappeared as she twirled out of the sari.

Marc's dark eyes gleamed when he saw she wore nothing under the sari. He quickly shucked off his clothes as she peeled off the tight-fitting blouse.

Amy felt his hands on her ribs before she was free of her blouse. She gasped as his heat nearly undid her. She felt her nipples tighten painfully. She had no idea that while she seduced him, her body was primed and ready for his touch.

Marc made good on his word to lick every inch of her, starting from her forehead down. By the time he made his way to her breasts, her skin tingled from the lightest touch. Each choppy breath she took hurt.

She had no idea how sensitive the crooks of her elbows were. The sight of him kneeling before her with his mouth on her flesh was more startling, more arousing than anything she imagined. When he dipped his tongue into her navel, a soft climax pulsed through her. She grabbed his hair in her fists and let out a soft cry. He held her up as her knees buckled.

"I have to have you now." His low, deep voice burred across her skin.

"But I haven't even tasted—"

"Now, Amy." He picked her up and strode to the settee. Rather than laying her along the length of the battered piece of furniture, she had to rest her head against the back as her hips and legs dangled off the cushion.

The raw masculinity in his face called to something deep and primal inside her. She wanted him to claim her with the ferocity she felt for him.

He entered her with one deep push. Amy arched off the settee as he pushed deeply into her core. Again and again before teasing her with a shallow thrust.

A growl emerged deep in her throat as her gold jewelry danced wildly. Desire glowed inside her as Marc continued to thrust, deep and measured. Her womb clenched when he surprised her with a slight buck.

He teased her with the shallow thrusts until she clawed and moaned, swaying and writhing for him. She saw the sheen of sweat glistening on his skin, the clustering of his muscles, the pain and pleasure dancing across his face.

Amy clenched around him, squeezing his cock and rendering him motionless. Marc gripped the back edge of the settee and drove deep into her, roaring with satisfaction as her hard climax triggered his.

White heat flashed across Amy's mind. For a moment, time was suspended and everything was silenced. And, just as quickly, sensations crashed upon her fast and furious.

She became dimly aware of Marc lying on top of her. He lifted his head away from her neck and moved to sit on the floor, taking Amy with him. She wearily straddled his hips as his cock nestled deep inside her.

The warmth from their joined bodies seeped through her, rising up to her heart. Marc cupped her face with his hands and looked deeply into her eyes.

"I love you, Amy." His voice was soft but clear.

She instinctively tried to duck her head, but he wouldn't let her look away. She felt too intensely. She felt too shy. She wasn't ready.

"I know." A wry smile tugged at his swollen mouth. "I shouldn't have said anything. It's too soon." He pressed his mouth against her and covered her lips with gentle kisses. "But I wanted you to know."

Amy closed her eyes as she savored the feel of him. She clutched his shoulder, refusing to break this bond, this moment. She loved Marc completely, but revealing it was a risk she wasn't sure she would ever be ready to make. Because this time, if he walked away from her, she would surely shatter.

Chapter 7

"You know what?" Amy asked Marc a week later as he held the glass door open and escorted her into the air-conditioned building. "I don't even want to attend this stupid party."

"Too late. People have seen us." He dipped his head and his faint cologne made her want to foam at the mouth. Marc placed a small kiss next to her ear. "Can't chicken out now," he whispered.

She huffed with resentment. "It's not about chickening out. This party isn't important anymore." Okay, she admitted to herself, some of that was true. The party didn't mean anything to her anymore. Chickening out might be a factor. A small one.

"Amy, stop stalling. We're going." He placed his hand on the small of her back and guided her down the corridor.

There were downsides of Marc understanding her and knowing what made her tick. But the good news was, she knew him just as intimately. She gave him a sly sideways glance, taking in his formal appearance. Wearing the dark suit, Marc looked powerful, almost ruthless. Amy could barely stand up straight whenever she looked at him.

Amy curled against his side and luxuriated in his body

heat. "I have a better idea on what to do this evening," she murmured.

His fingers flexed against her spine, the only indication that she was getting to him. "Good. Hold that thought. Anticipation makes it sweeter."

The rat. She'd give him anticipation. "But Marc," she answered with an innocent smile, "don't you remember that I'm not wearing anything underneath this dress? Are you sure you want the never-before and possible never-again event to go to waste?"

Indecision and hot desire flickered in his eyes. His expression tightened as if he was suffering silently. "Smile, sweetheart," he finally said through gritted teeth. "You're about to make your grand entrance."

Amy stepped away from Marc and straightened her shoulders. She took a deep breath as her stomach flipped and rolled. She instinctively sought out Marc's hand and found the peace she was looking for. The wattage in her smile increased as he meshed his fingers with hers and held on tight.

She didn't know what she was worried about. Maybe because she wore a slinky orange cocktail dress that required one to "work" and "commit" to or look foolish. It didn't help that she teamed the knock-'em-dead dress with sky-high heels that would make a foot fetishist weep for mercy.

But she had nothing to worry about. Marc was at her side. Nothing could go wrong. Of course, completing her Other Woman ensemble with the guy who could make her hot and wet simultaneously was problematic. A guy whom she loved to distraction. A guy who was way out of her league—everyone in the room would know that.

A few guests by the door had already spotted her. The slack jaws and bugged eyes were flattering as much as they were nerve-wracking. After she shared a glance with her conspirator, Amy crossed the threshold with Marc and stepped into the crowded ballroom. The whispers, nods and knowing looks rippled across the room.

In all the scenarios Amy had considered, she always imagined the scene from *Gone with the Wind* where Scarlett attends Ashley's birthday party all vamped up. Melanie, played by Tanya, would pale in comparison. Of course, the daydreams conveniently ended before she remembered that Melanie's graciousness saved the day.

"Amy. You're here." Tanya suddenly appeared before them. Amy's confidence took a nosedive. The blonde didn't look anything like dreary Melanie Wilkes.

Tanya looked like a goddess. Her fire-engine-red dress was skintight, plunging down and hiking up to show off her body to the best advantage. With curves that would make beauty queens envious, Amy didn't know why she could have pulled a stunt like this. She must have been completely delusional.

She wanted to curl into Marc. Hide. Disappear. Marc proved to be immovable and kept her at his side. He probably planned it, Amy decided. He was going to pay dearly for that.

"Hello, Tanya." *It's not a competition . . . it's not a competition . . . Especially when it's obvious that you are going to lose.* "You look wonderful."

Tanya blinked her expensive mink eyelashes and frowned, obviously trying to figure out where the slam was in that statement. "Thanks."

"And do you know Dr. Marc Javier?" She gestured to Marc. Why were her good-girl tendencies kicking in? She was about ready to have it out with the office slut. It was like going to a catfight armed with elbow-length kid gloves.

Tanya's eyes narrowed at the title. "Hi, Marc." As if she took offense to what she didn't have—or wasn't marrying. "I didn't realize you two were together."

"Yes, we are," Marc answered. Then he looked down at Amy. The heated look made her feel desired and cherished. She wondered if she was glowing.

"Uh-huh." Tanya flipped her hair behind her shoulder. "Well, you'll have to excuse me. I need to mingle with my guests."

"Of course," Amy murmured, startled by the other woman's quick retreat. That was it? She worked hard for six weeks and all she got was a lousy "uh-huh"?

Amy watched Tanya leave. She felt relieved. Let down. Confused. "That wasn't so bad after all," she told Marc out of the side of her mouth.

"It's because you used the element of surprise," he answered as he led her into the crowded room, his fingers tangled with hers. "She didn't expect you to show up—with a date, and looking unbelievably sexy. Not a good combination when you happen to be her fiancé's ex-girlfriend." His grasp tightened painfully for an instant.

"She'll live." Amy didn't care about Tanya's reaction. She wanted to hear more on his opinion that she was unbelievably sexy.

"Don't think she'll take it lightly." He let go of her hand and grabbed two flutes of champagne from a waiter passing by. "Give her fifteen minutes and she'll come back with a full attack."

"You are really getting into this, aren't you?" Amy asked dryly as she accepted her glass.

"Just making sure no one messes with my woman." He scanned the room as Amy tingled all over from his possessiveness. "Now why haven't we seen Kevin?"

The champagne bubbles on her tongue went flat at the mention of Kevin. "He's probably networking. Which is what you should be doing."

"No, I'd rather be with you."

"You'll be with me after the party," she reminded him

as her blood fizzed in her veins. Amy stepped away from Marc before she acted on her impulses. She glanced around the room. "See, there's your boss right there. He's waving you over."

"Shit." Marc turned abruptly and blocked Amy's view of the elderly gentleman.

"Come on, Marc." She obviously needed to teach him a few schmoozing techniques. "What's the harm in talking to him for a few minutes? He probably would love to hear about your sensuality project. Want to show off your best case study?" She struck a pose.

He paled. "Amy, I never thought of you as a case study," he said earnestly.

"That's *so* sweet."

"No," he shook his head, "you don't understand. I should have told you sooner. Right at the beginning. But I knew you would be hurt."

Worry gnawed at her stomach. "Tell me what?"

He looked into her eyes and wouldn't look away. "You have every right to be angry at me."

The worry was graduating into a sickening dread. "I'm going to get angrier by the minute if you don't tell me what this is all about."

"The sensuality project. You were never in it." Marc winced as if he expected to be attacked by flying objects. "You weren't a good candidate," he hurriedly continued, "but I knew you wouldn't handle getting rejected from the group so I made up your course."

"Anything else?" she asked cautiously.

"No. Now let me have it," he said grimly.

"All I can say is . . ." She shrugged. "Duh!"

Marc flinched. His mouth sagged open. "You knew?" he barked out. The people near them glanced over at them. "When?" he continued in a whisper.

"Right around the second week when the salon put my

feet in a warm paraffin masque." She took another sip of her champagne. "It didn't make sense why pedicures were on the syllabus for becoming an intimate communicator."

Marc drew back and studied her. "You're not mad at me?" he asked with disbelief.

"Why would I be? I'm eternally grateful to you. Not only did you introduce me to the joys of getting a massage, but you also went out of your way to help me."

"Excuse me, miss." Marc's boss appeared at her side. "I've been trying to get a hold of your man for quite some time. Javier,"—he clapped his hand on Marc's solid shoulder—"come talk to these gentlemen about your project."

My man. Yeah, she liked the sounds of that. "Go ahead," she answered magnanimously. "I have a few people I need to say hello to."

Marc looked around the ballroom. Amy was nowhere to be found. The problem was, he couldn't find Kevin, either.

He'd like to think he was a logical person. That the two events were merely coincidences. But he knew that Amy in her full glory would be irresistible to Kevin.

Marc walked around the perimeter of the room, trying not to look like he misplaced his date. He was not going to growl at every guest. He wouldn't tear the room apart looking for Amy.

He'd give himself five more minutes and then all bets were off.

As he walked by the glass doors leading out to the garden, a movement caught his eye. He jerked his head back and saw a flash of orange disappear behind a tree. *Amy.* Marc then saw the gleam of blond hair above where the orange had been. *With Kevin.*

The momentary relief congealed into jealousy so thick, Marc wanted to puke. He strode into the garden before he thought about it. He knew Amy wasn't interested in Kevin, but he couldn't get rid of the fear stuck in his throat. Because he didn't know if Amy said she wasn't interested in Kevin because she couldn't have him.

"You look really hot, Amy."

Marc imagined Kevin's smarmy smile. His footsteps smashed the grass as he headed for the tree.

"So you've said," she replied dryly. "Thank you."

Marc skidded to a stop. Amy sounded less than thrilled to talk to Kevin. Almost inconvenienced. As much as the need to interrupt shimmered through his muscles, Marc knew he had to let Amy handle it.

"Why didn't you dress up like that when we were together?" Kevin asked.

Marc shook his head and leaned against a tall bush next to him. He didn't need to interfere. Kevin was digging his own grave.

"Why does it matter?" Amy replied coolly. "I didn't want to. I didn't feel like it at the time."

"And now you do. Because you want me back."

Marc glared at the tree. He didn't like how Kevin's voice dropped into a seductive tone.

Amy's exasperated huff echoed in the garden. "Why does everybody think I'm trying to get you back?"

"It's okay, Amy. I feel the same way about you."

Marc's fingers curled into a tight fist. This was not looking good. Where was the kiss-off he imagined?

"You . . . want me back?"

Her dazed tone ate away at Marc. He should have interrupted when he had the chance. Damn it, when was he going to learn?

"Yeah." Kevin positively purred. "I want you, Amy."

Marc shattered inside. The determination to fight oozed out of him. He felt empty. Broken.

"A fine time to decide that during your engagement party."

"Huh? What does that have to do—"

"Oh, I get it." Amy's brittle voice carried across the

garden. "It's not either me or Tanya. It's both. You want me on the side. Sneak behind Tanya's back."

"Babe, you got it all wrong."

"Good, because I'm not interested in dating you ever again."

Marc lifted his head. A glimmer of hope stirred to life. Amy really didn't have any interest in her ex.

"Who's talking about dating?" Kevin sounded like the dazed and confused one now. "I'm talking threesomes."

Time wavered in the stilled silence. Marc slowly straightened, ready to push Kevin into a nearby bush. Preferably one with sharp thorns.

"No thanks, Kevin." Icicles could have formed on her words. "I'm in love with Marc."

Marc almost slid into the bush. He caught himself before he got a mouthful of dirt. Amy loved him? Maybe he was hallucinating. Hearing what he wanted to hear.

"Love? Amy, what does that have to do with anything? This is about sex."

"Let me rephrase that. I'm happy with Marc. I don't want to look outside of the bedroom for someone else."

"Yeah?" Kevin scoffed. "How long do you think that'll last?"

"Probably forever."

Amy's certainty eased the tightness in Marc's chest. She was in love with him? A smile tugged at his mouth. The forever kind. And when the hell was she going to inform him of that?

"You're crazy." Kevin's voice hardened. "You've dated him for what? A week? A month?"

"When you know, you know," Amy answered wearily. "And I know you should go back inside to your engagement party."

Once she was alone, Amy sagged against the tree and closed her eyes. What had she ever seen in Kevin? She shook her head wearily. Why had she wasted so much time and emotion over that guy?

"You should have punched him."

She gasped. "Marc!" Amy whirled and saw him lounging against the other side of the trunk. Realization hit her with a whomp. "You heard everything?"

"Just the juicy parts."

Amy frowned. "And you didn't hit him?"

"I'm considering it," Marc said as he walked around to Amy's side, "but I thought that honor should go to you."

"Mighty generous of you," she replied, watching him cautiously, unable to read his mood.

"But you let the guy leave without a scratch," he teased. "Have you learned nothing from me?"

"I'm conserving my energy for us later tonight."

"Good answer." He leaned his shoulder against the wood and fell silent. Amy's heart pounded harder as every second passed, wondering what he was going to say. She gnawed her lip as he drew in a breath.

"*Ménage à trois*, huh?"

Amy cringed. Of all the things to ask about. . . . She felt the flush warm her face. "I don't see him convincing Tanya with that idea," she muttered.

"Are you interested in one?"

His gruff tone made her look at him sharply. "No, I want only you." She was amazed that she wasn't shy saying it. She actually felt braver. "Always."

"Might find that boring after a while," he warned, his eyes intent on her. "My ex-wife did." There was no bitterness in his voice, only reservation.

Amy slid her arms over his shoulders, her heart thumping against her breastbone. "She didn't love you like I do," she said and kissed him.

Her nervousness evaporated the moment her lips touched his. He greedily accepted her kiss and overwhelmed her with a passion that stole her breath. She knew the strength of her feelings matched his love for her. The knowledge made her feel brazen. Invincible.

The kiss was meant to seal her vow and Amy pulled away, but couldn't deny herself his touch. She kissed him again and again until the fast and furious kisses melted into something deep and toe-curling. A tantalizing longing pressed and swelled between her thighs.

Marc seemed to know exactly how her body responded. He cupped her breast, thumbing her hard nipple through the thin layer of her dress. Amy shuddered, her hitching breath raw against the faint party music.

Amy's hands slid from his jacket and pressed against his crisp linen shirt. She felt his pounding heart under her palms. Her fingers curled with impatience, bunching his shirt in her fists.

"Let me take you home," Marc whispered roughly. "To bed. *Now.*"

She didn't think she would last that long. To her, "now" meant before leaving the garden. The idea gave a kick to her heated blood. Could she seduce him right here, right now?

"Don't you remember what you said before we arrived?" Amy leaned against the tree and closed her eyes, needing to tease. Torment. "Anticipation makes it sweeter."

She stroked her cheekbones and jaw with her fingertips. Marc covered her hands with his. "Don't touch," she ordered huskily as her thumb dragged against her parted lips, tugging the plump, rosy flesh. "Watch."

"Uh . . . Amy—I—wh—oh." Marc's voice was raspy as she caressed her arched throat before she splayed her fingers against her chest. Her mouth tilted in a small smile. He was already affected by her performance. Was she really that powerful? That desirable?

She opened her eyes and boldly met his heated gaze. Amy hesitated when she saw his lopsided grin. She broke eye contact. That wasn't the reaction she was trying to achieve.

Did she look stupid? Was she crazy for risking getting caught?

Amy looked at him again and relief crashed through her. Marc stared at her with awe. He understood the significance of her actions. Not only was she giving herself pleasure, but she was also doing it for his eyes only.

Amy massaged her breasts, arching her spine as she grasped her stiff nipples. She tweaked and plucked, enjoying the pull of desire. Her hands smoothed down her stomach before her fingertips feathered her curls between her legs. She hesitated. Her body was desperate for her touch. She wanted to do it in front of Marc, but felt vulnerable.

His hands grasped her waist, his long fingers kneading her flesh. "Don't stop," he insisted. Pleaded.

She found it difficult to speak. Swallow. Breathe. "Why don't you take over?"

"Nah." The tremors sweeping through his body were at odds with his casual words. His mouth pressed against her ear. "I want to watch."

Her skin tingled at the raw statement. "But . . ."

He shoved the hem of her dress to her hips, the fabric mashed in his fists. "I want to watch you pleasure yourself. Let me see what you like. Show me," he growled.

Her skin flared with renewed heat. She moved one hand to her breast, pinching her furled nipple. She mewled and her other hand moved down and cupped the downy apex of her thighs.

Marc nuzzled the soft spot behind her ear. "Oh, God, you don't know what you're doing to me," he murmured. "I want you bad."

Her hand grazed the curls, softly at first. Up and down. Back and forth. Her touch didn't alleviate the building intensity. It heightened it. Sharpened it. Desire bubbled in the curves and crevices of her body, frothing and foaming, through her blood.

Amy bathed in Marc's body heat. With a quick sideways look, her gaze locked with his. He appeared fascinated by the expressions flitting across her face.

Her fingers met with the dewy evidence of her arousal. Her breath quickened. She parted her legs wider and rested heavily against the trunk as her fingers slid and dipped. Desire swirled and spiraled from her chest to her abdomen, tightening around her pelvis. Her eyes fluttered closed as the beginnings of a climax rippled through her muscles.

"Oh . . . Marc . . ." she whispered.

"I'm here." His lips moved against the delicate shell of her ear.

She gasped as the first wave of her climax peaked to another level. "Touch me," she whimpered urgently.

Marc's hand immediately covered hers. His fingers combed through the curls that hid her most intimate treasure. Amy's desire climbed to a new level as Marc pleasured her. He dipped between and rubbed her slick flesh the same way she showed him. Amy moaned and writhed under his hand.

"More," she mouthed, her eyes clenched tight as she surrendered to the fiery sensations. Her eyes flashed open as Marc pressed the pearl hidden behind the folds.

"Marc!" she cried out as her body erupted from the intense pleasure. She grabbed onto his shoulders, searching for something solid to hold onto. His mouth came crashing down on hers as the howling storm of sensations caught her, mind, body and soul.

After the roar consumed her body, Amy heard nothing. Slowly, she became aware of her heart thumping wildly. She heard her choppy breaths before the light strains of chamber music and party chatter invaded her mind.

"Let's ditch this party," Marc whispered in her ear. He stepped away, his reluctance in letting go almost tangible. Her knees wanted to cave in from the absence of his warmth and strong hold.

"I'm all for it. But there is one more thing I have to do." It was past time. No more excuses.

"Punch Kevin?" he asked hopefully.

She laughed as she smoothed her dress. "No."

"Dunk Tanya in the punch bowl? Start a food fight?"

"Nope." She walked away from the tree and stood in the middle of the garden before she crooked her finger at him. "Dance with me."

"Really?" His voice caught in his throat. He moved toward her in a daze. "I thought you didn't know how."

"It's true." She linked her hands behind his neck. Nestling close to his body, her body yearned for his hardness. "I don't know how. You'll have to teach me." She rested her head on his shoulder.

Marc's arms tightened around her. "With pleasure."

CODE PINK

Chapter 1

$3^?,5*9l5*73^.3^'0$7#;0,7^?*;0l5.*0W57l%9*7}39l'^*
?l35*.7^$07**33k/392'5/.<0*..007[/39$5^[7?9,0*;7.3^0
39*W00*W05**;01789,0.*59,5^*%0[3,010t3^i?;**;0#,7!
0/395^'W07^569-0^^7[0,

Jennifer Clark smiled with satisfaction. It was perfect. A masterpiece. It was her best code yet.

She took a salutary sip of white wine although it was probably too early to congratulate herself. She had ten minutes to go, but victory was certain. If Robert hadn't figured out the code by now, he wasn't going to.

Because she was the best. A flush of pride swept through her. No one was going to top her. Not when it came to codes. Breaking or building them.

Jennifer tucked the paper into her cluttered purse and her fingers brushed up against Amy Bryce's wedding invitation. The heady glow instantly disappeared as her heart squeezed with regret. She was thrilled to see her sorority sister find true love, but it wasn't too long ago that Jennifer had been naively planning for her own wedding.

She couldn't think about that. Jennifer determinedly straightened her spine. She was moving on. Maybe with Robert. He met all of her requirements: smart, good-looking and wanted her more than anything else. Most importantly, he was the antithesis of Bryan.

Checking her watch one more time, Jennifer decided she'd been a good sport long enough. She knew Robert wouldn't decipher the code in time. No one could.

Jennifer signed the bill and took one last sip of her drink as a movement caught her eye. She glanced at the doorway and promptly gagged on her wine.

Slapping her hand against her mouth, she choked the liquid down before it squirted out of her nose. It was difficult not spluttering it all back up as Special Agent Bryan Matthews spotted her.

Bryan. Matthews. The name flashed before her like neon lights. Bryan. The Love of Her Life. The Best Sex She Ever Had. Also commonly known as The Man Who Broke Her Heart And STOMPED On It While He Was At It.

He strode into the restaurant, blatantly disregarding the no jacket, no service rule. The well-worn fisherman sweater, faded jeans and scuffed boots blared against the Federal décor. Each step he took was slow and measured, but it felt like he was crashing through the Limoges china and equestrian artwork.

Yet Bryan Matthews wasn't one to draw attention to himself. He was designed to skulk, to glide around the edges. When he chose to cross open spaces, it was to attack. To capture his prey.

And she was his prey tonight. Her skin prickled with alarm. She stared at him silently, noting the streaks of golden brown in his thick black hair. His hair used to fall past his chin in untamed waves. Now it was cropped close, emphasizing the aggressive curves of his skull.

His skin was bronzed and weathered, the lines etched deeper in his face. Even his dark eyes seemed to slice through her defenses and see exactly what she wanted to hide. This Bryan Matthews was leaner, sleeker. Deadlier to her senses.

She didn't know how she managed to conjure him up.

At the moment, she didn't care. All she wanted was to banish him from her existence.

Bryan sat down in the empty chair at her table. "Jennifer," he said in his slightly rasping voice that could still make her shiver.

It was a struggle not to rub her hands over her bare forearms. "That seat is taken," she replied calmly as she felt her pulse flutter in her throat.

The edge of his mouth kicked up into a knowing smile. "No, it's not. How have you been?"

"Fine, up until this moment." She instinctively crossed her legs tighter, the stroke of silk stockings against her thighs doing nothing to stop her trembling. "What are you doing here? Make a wrong turn on the fast track?"

"No, I'm waiting for a new assignment. What have you been up to?" He reached for her wine glass and downed the contents.

The sight of the fragile crystal in his big, masculine hand had a mesmerizing effect. "What do you want, Bryan? Say what you have to say and then get moving. I'm waiting for someone."

He set the glass down. "Yeah, I know. Robert." He grimaced at the name.

The back of her neck tingled with warning. She couldn't imagine Robert saying anything to Bryan. "How did you know that?"

"Like you really expected him to show up."

Her glare deepened. He knew something, but she wasn't going to give him the pleasure of watching her squirm. Jennifer went on the offensive. "Not *everyone* dumps me."

Annoyance flashed through Bryan's slate gray eyes. "Get it straight, Jennifer. You dumped me."

Jennifer cocked one eyebrow but said nothing in her defense. She knew it was useless.

"So what's going on between you and Robert?" Bryan asked. The thrust of his chin signaled his leashed anger.

"That's none of your business." She grabbed her purse and pushed her chair back.

"It is now."

Jennifer froze. Damn, she hated when he used that voice. She hated when he knew something she didn't. "What are you talking about?"

"This." He pulled the creased paper from the front pocket of his jeans and tossed it on the table. It skittered in front of her. Her eyes widened as she read the decoded message she'd sent to Robert.

Congratulations on deciphering the last e-mail, but you shouldn't gloat since it took you 2 days. Let's see if you can figure this one out. Meet me at the 1789 Restaurant before 10 tonight. The prize? You and me in a 69. Jennifer

She felt the earth dip and slant. Every emotion slammed and boomeranged inside her. "How did you get this?" She barely croaked the words out.

"You're missing the point." Bryan lounged back in his seat. "I deciphered it before ten. And I'm here for my prize."

Bryan watched her with a hunger that threatened to consume him. He wanted nothing more than to swoop down, take her back to his bed and remind her why they should be together.

"So tell me," he said, striving for a conversational tone, "did you offer the sixty-nine position because it's a fantasy of yours, or because it made the code more difficult?" He was betting on the latter. Praying for it, because he was going to be really pissed if she hadn't wanted to share that fantasy with him.

Jennifer crumpled the paper in her hand and stuffed it in her purse. "What do you want?"

"I think it's obvious."

She reluctantly made eye contact. "You aren't getting a

sixty-nine. At least not from me." She rose from her seat. "Goodbye, Bryan."

He guzzled in the sight of her. The black cocktail dress made her appear more delicate and defenseless, but he knew better. He also knew that oh-so-proper dress hid her fondness for pastel lingerie. It would be made from the most sumptuous silk and fringed with lace that always tore under his eager fingers.

"I broke the code in time," he reminded her, wanting to get back to the matter at hand while his mind imprinted the sight of a rose teddy against her sweat-slicked skin.

"The offer wasn't made to you and you know it." She marched to the exit without a backwards glance.

He was at her side before she made it to the door. "That wasn't specified," he murmured in her ear. She smelled good. The sweet floral scent kicked him right in the groin and his dick stirred with interest. "The offer could have been for anyone."

She turned and glared at him, her blond hair swinging away from her face. "What were you doing with Robert's e-mail anyway?"

Her diamond stud earrings snagged his attention and hope roared into his chest. He gave those to her last Christmas. "You're getting off-topic here," he said. "You want to welsh on the deal."

"I'm not welshing, because the deal wasn't made for you," she said as she retrieved her coat.

"Why are you playing games with Robert?" He took the coat from her grasp and held it out for her. "You could do so much better."

"Better as in you?" She stuffed her arms into the black wool sleeve and stepped away from him.

"You said it, not me."

"Robert isn't threatened by the fact that I am a better code-breaker than him," she said as she buttoned her coat with fierce, angry movements. "He actually finds that a turn-on."

Robert was going to get his face punched in, Bryan thought but that was beside the point. "You mean you're not threatened by his talent. Like you are with me."

"I'm not threatened by you," she said as she gave inordinate attention to putting on leather gloves.

He snorted at the bald-faced lie. "Bull."

Her head jerked up and she glared at him, her blue eyes flashing fire. "Because I am better than you."

Bryan braced his legs like a gunslinger at a showdown. "I have the results of a cryptanalysis exam that says otherwise."

Jennifer rolled her eyes. "One lousy exam."

"That lousy exam gave me a promotion." He rocked back on his boots. "Over you."

"Newsflash. I'm now at the same level as you," she revealed before bestowing him a snippy closed-mouth smile.

"Congratulations, but I was there first." Not to mention he tested his abilities every day while she wasted away as a manager in the Encryption Department. He despised the fact that she hid in an office where she reigned supreme. And he hated the idea that he might be responsible for her sudden lack of adventure.

"So what?" Jennifer tossed back. "The exam proves nothing."

He slid his hands in his back pockets. "Wanna bet?"

"No!" She gave her gloves a final tug. "You've been known to cheat."

"Not when it comes to you."

She looked straight in his eyes and quickly looked away. "Tell that to someone who cares," Jennifer said, and walked out with her chin tilted high.

She sensed Bryan next to her on the sidewalk before she saw him from the corner of her eye. Her sigh was thick with aggravation. "Why are you following me?"

"Well, there's that promise of a sixty-nine," he said, hunching his shoulders against the cold November night.

"For the last time," she said through clenched teeth. "I'm not doing it."

He shrugged. "Okay, fine."

Now that's suspicious. "Fine?"

"Yeah, fine. You can substitute it."

She took a prudent step away from him. "With what?"

"A new wager."

"I seriously don't like the sound of this." Or maybe it was that sly gleam in his eyes that had her on guard.

He took a step toward her. "I'm going to prove to you once and for all that I'm the better codebreaker."

"Oh, this is going to be good." She folded her arms across her chest, prepared to be dazzled.

"You send me a code. No." He shook his head as he changed his mind. "Three codes that I have to break in a reasonable timeframe."

Jennifer's eyebrows dipped in disbelief. "And why would I want to do that?"

"If I break all three codes, then you have to admit that I'm the best. In public."

She waited a beat. Then two. "And, I repeat, why would I want to do that?"

"But if I can't crack one, then I leave you alone."

Tempting. She pursed her lips. "Define alone."

"I won't see you outside the office and while we're at work, I'll keep it at a professional level."

Yeah, right. Bryan hadn't been professional with her from the first moment they had met across a conference table and he had propositioned her. But she couldn't figure out his game. "And when I win, you'll shut up about the exam?"

He considered it for a moment. "Sure." His breath came out as a puff in the cold air.

Hmmm.... "Even if you crack one and it's not on time?"

"Yep."

It was too good to be true. He was definitely up to something and she wasn't going to fall for it again. Or fall for *him* again. "No, thanks." Jennifer whirled around and headed down the sidewalk. "I'll pass."

Chapter 2

Bryan couldn't believe it. She didn't take the bet. That was impossible. He saw that flare of interest in her eyes. Why did she refuse to play?

"Chicken!" he called out to her.

She stopped and cast a withering glare over her shoulder. "Oh, that's mature. For your information, I don't have time to play games."

"Yeah, you do. That's why you've been sending codes to Robert. You're looking for a challenge. Some fun. And why not? Your job is way beneath your abilities. I can tell you're bored out of your mind."

"That's because I'm listening to you."

He shrugged and leaned against the building. "Give me three good reasons why you can't take the bet."

"I don't have to give you any reasons," Jennifer said and started walking again. "Bye, Bryan."

"Because you can't come up with any?"

"Because I don't feel like it," she said without looking back.

"Fine, I'll answer for you."

She tossed her arms in the air with exasperation. "Don't you have something better to do? Like play in traffic?"

"Number one, your codebreaking skills are rusty."

Jennifer skidded to a halt and whirled around. Her eyes were wide with disbelief as she stomped back to him, her slender heels clipping against the concrete. "They are not! Take that back. Take that back this instant!"

"I just broke one of your codes," he reminded her. "Not your best work." It still managed to cramp his brain, but she didn't need to know that.

Jennifer's nostrils flared as she tried to rein in her temper. "You don't know what you're talking about."

"Two," he continued, ticking the number off with his fingers, "you can't handle the idea of losing. Again. Especially losing to me. Again."

She raised her hands and froze before balling her fingers into fists. "Again . . . I didn't lose. You cheated."

He narrowed his eyes in warning. "Keep telling yourself that if it makes you happy, but we both know the truth."

She flinched. Whether it was with surprise or guilt, he couldn't be sure. Jennifer flipped her hair out of her eyes and nailed him with a haughty glare. "That's only two reasons."

"Three," he continued evenly, "you're afraid of us."

She scrunched her nose. "Us?"

"Yeah, you still feel what's going on between us."

She looked away. "Nothing's going on."

He caught her chin with his hand and firmly drew her attention back where it belonged. "You don't feel the pull? The heat?" He'd put up with a lot of bull from her, but he wouldn't let her deny this.

She brushed his hand off. "You mean the early symptoms I get before the dry heaves? You feel it, too? I had no idea it was contagious."

"So you do feel something." He pointed out smugly.

"Bryan, only you would feel triumphant about making me nauseous."

"Babe, I make you feel a lot of things." His raspy voice

cut through the cold like a whip. "Nausea ain't one of them."

"Let's see. Headache, the tic in my eye . . ."

"Lust." He quickly pulled her into the shadows. "Desire. Need."

Jennifer batted at his hands. "What do you think you're doing?" she said in a growl as he guided her between his legs.

"Shutting you up." He couldn't ignore how good it felt to have her against him again. Cupping the back of her head, his fingers crushed her silky hair. The moment Bryan pressed his mouth against hers, he realized his mistake.

Kissing Jennifer should come with a warning. It was like taking medication while operating heavy machinery. It muddled his senses and set his body on edge.

To his surprise, Jennifer showed no resistance. She softened under his mouth, but that didn't sate his hunger. It reminded him how famished he was for her touch.

His chest clenched as she parted her lips and drew him in. She tasted just as he remembered. His body thrummed with need. He wanted to devour her. Inhale her.

Jennifer stiffened against him, as if she had just remembered why she shouldn't kiss him. His arms flexed, unwilling to let her go. She wrenched her mouth from his. Bringing a gloved hand to her swollen lips, she stared at him with narrowed eyes. "Are you through?"

"I don't know. How chatty do you feel right now?" Bryan felt just as disoriented as Jennifer acted. He watched her stumble back, his reactions dulled and sluggish as he fought the need to drag her back into his arms.

"You know what?" she said as she drew to her full height. "I'll take that bet."

Bryan arched his eyebrow. "Can't get enough of me?"

"I can't get *away from you* fast enough," Jennifer corrected him, feeling out of sorts. Damn, he had kissed her good. Her ears were still buzzing from it. "The sooner I win this bet, the sooner you are out of my life."

"Wow. Feel the love."

She shoved her hands in her hair and dragged her fingers through the tangles. "This is probably the stupidest thing I've ever done." She paused and allowed her gaze to drift from Bryan's head to his boots. "No, make that second stupidest thing."

Bryan's hooded eyes masked his emotions. "I'm not even going to ask."

"Smart of you." She placed her hands on her hips. "Okay, here are the terms."

"Since when are you in charge?"

"I'm always in charge," she informed him. "I'm e-mailing three codes to you this week. Each code requires you to be somewhere at a certain time."

"Somewhere in DC, right?"

"Yeah, I do have a full-time job, you know."

"Just checking. I wouldn't put it past you to send me to Siberia."

"Why would I do that?" she asked with pseudo-sweetness. "I have to be at these locations to prove that you didn't crack the code on time."

"Then I might as well tail you."

"No, because that would be cheating. And if I find out you cheated, I win by default. And . . ." And what? She had nothing to keep him in line. "And you have to admit that I'm the best. In front of the entire Encryption Department."

"Fine. Same to you." He leaned his head against the brick wall.

"Fine." She folded her arms across her chest. His relaxed pose set her on edge. He looked way too satisfied.

"If you cheat, I win," Bryan said.

"I never cheat."

"Let me rephrase that. If you don't display good sportsmanship, then I win by default and you give me a sixty-nine."

Her eyes bugged out. "In front of the Encryption Department?"

A grin tugged at the edge of his mouth. "I wouldn't go that far."

"What is it with you and this sixty-nine?" she asked, aggravation burring her words. It had nothing to do with his sexy smile. Nothing at all.

"Why didn't you offer it to me when we were dating?" he tossed back, his eyes glittering.

"Because I knew better." She swallowed awkwardly and cleared her throat. "So do we have a deal?"

He dragged his gaze down her length and back up. "Yeah, we have a deal."

She tried to ignore how her skin flushed and tightened in response. "Expect an e-mail from me tomorrow morning."

"Can't wait."

His confidence, his lack of concern bugged her. "Can't wait to lose?"

His eyelids drifted closed. "I'm not going to."

"Are you kidding?" She felt compelled to tweak at him. "You're going down."

His smile widened. "Only on you."

Chapter 3

%???7%?;27>?71%#$&?28 ~7/@%?/1?-*?$$(/?9

Jennifer studied the twenty monkeys dangling from the ceiling of the Arthur M. Sackler Gallery, wondering why she was going through this. She had nothing to prove. Especially to Bryan.

She had other things to do like restarting a life, which was turning into a job similar to cleaning out a closet. It took more time and created more of a mess than anyone ever anticipated.

And as she would when cleaning closets, she dragged her feet on the chore until it was absolutely necessary. Only when she saw Bryan did she realize how much she allowed life to slide by. How much she distanced herself from the excitement she found in the world of cryptanalysis.

Putting together the code for Bryan was more fun than she had had in a long time. She missed the kick of energy, the thrill bubbling in her veins. She didn't get nearly the same kind of buzz at work these days.

But she was going to change that. Today she placed a request for a new assignment. It didn't matter whether she won or lost this wager with Bryan—and she would win.

But now she wanted to find something tougher at work. Something more challenging. Fun.

She wasn't sure why codes were fun. She had always loved anything to do with secret languages and symbols. She saw codes in anything, anytime, anywhere. Everyone had found that peculiar. That is, everyone but her sorority sisters and Bryan.

Jennifer glanced up, looking for Bryan at the top of the steps. No sign of him and he had five minutes left. She could breathe a little easier. He wasn't going to show. *Please don't let him show.*

She leaned her head against the wall and stared at the monkey chain. Was Bryan still working on her code or had he given up? And was it so wrong to wish that he was suffering? She hoped not—simply for the fact that she didn't like being in the wrong.

She also couldn't help but enjoy the vision of her code sending him into fits. Picturing him in a fetal position and blubbering away like an idiot. Making him regret thinking that he was better than she.

Bryan didn't need to know that encrypting and deciphering were the only talents she had. Or how much she struggled at being the best at it. Jennifer had desperately wanted to be the best of something. It didn't take long for her to come to the conclusion she would never be the smartest, prettiest, fastest or even the most successful.

Even these days when she went to her alma mater, the only thing people remembered was how she had been the class know-it-all. Not exactly something she wanted to be remembered by. She wanted to be memorable on something cool. Something that no one could come close to.

And how was she ever going to be the best, become something of a legend, at her present job? You can't set the world on fire being safe and over-qualified, she thought. You can't be the best. Only . . . obsolete.

But not for long. And she would never let Bryan know

that she stumbled on her way to becoming a legend. Jennifer squeezed her eyes shut, trying to will away the image of him that seemed permanently etched in her mind, but it was no use. Even on the day she met him, she saw all of her fears thrown together in a sexy package. The guy was too clever, too handsome, too dangerous, and way too good at cryptanalysis.

So of course she fell for him. Jennifer shook her head in self-disgust as she opened her eyes. He was her competitor. Her adversary. And finally, her equal.

While everyone had said she was the best, she had always feared that it wouldn't last long. How long was the question. Bryan managed to smash her worst-case prediction to smithereens. She had anticipated that she would be left behind eventually, just not so soon. And she hadn't been prepared that it would have hurt this badly.

A hand blurred past her face. Jennifer yelped in surprise. She turned and her gaze collided with gray eyes. Gloating gray eyes.

"Bryan?" Her voice came out in a squawk.

"Surprised? You shouldn't be."

She took a hurried look at her watch. He had two minutes to spare. "How did you—when—uh . . ."

"Babe, I might be the best damn codebreaker, but I have no clue what you're trying to say."

He didn't even look like he had to break a sweat deciphering her message. No gray sprouting in his thick hair. No new worry lines marring his tanned, lean face. Hell, not even a crease in his designer sweatshirt and faded jeans. How did he do it?

"Are you getting help from other people in Encryption?" She narrowed her eyes with suspicion. "If so, then that's unfair."

"I didn't need help in breaking that code. You obviously have a thing for numbers. Twenty monkeys"—he gestured to the ceiling above—"four P.M."—he pointed to her watch—"You have twenty-four hours," Bryan mimic-ked and rolled his eyes. "Babe, you even did the date in numbers."

"Is that a complaint?" Jennifer wasn't going to tolerate Bryan critiquing her work. She pivoted on her heel and headed for the nearest corridor. She needed to leave before she did or said something stupid. "Fine, no numbers next time. Guaranteed."

"Was that the best you could do?" Bryan was at her side, matching her pace.

Jennifer gritted her teeth. For someone who claimed to be a hotshot codebreaker, couldn't he see the signs that he was pushing his luck?

" 'Cause if it is," Bryan continued, "we might as well call me the winner right now."

She scoffed at the very idea. "I don't think so." She had to get away from Bryan. Regroup. Rethink her strategy.

"Why not? I don't think you're trying very hard."

Jennifer stomped her foot. "Oh, enough already."

"No, I'm serious." He caught her arm and stood in front of her, blocking her escape. "You don't see me as a threat. You can't believe that I'm your equal."

Jennifer shrugged him off her arm. "Well . . ."

"Your superior."

He went too far. "Now you're talking crazy." She re-sumed her search for the quickest exit. Seeing a doorway that looked promising, she made a dive for it.

Jennifer skidded to a stop when the possible exit turned out to be yet another alcove. There was nothing there but three walls, a bench, and carefully positioned overhead light-ing. Terrific. What was the point of that? Whoever designed the building had some explaining to do.

"Then tell me this," Bryan said from right behind her.

Her shoulders sagged. She might as well treat him like the troll at the bridge and answered the damn question so she could pass. "What?"

"Why did you blow off the exam?"

She froze, her bones suddenly feeling brittle. Her lungs squeezed shut as her blood stilled. "Huh?" She barely heard her voice over the pounding in her ears.

"The exam for the promotion." Bryan's raspy voice softened with anger. "You purposely failed it."

Her mouth sagged open and she slowly met his cold gaze. "How do you know about that?"

Bryan didn't know that he had been hoping he was wrong until her confession. Why couldn't she have denied it? Proven him wrong?

"It was obvious," Bryan answered. "What isn't obvious is *why* you cheated."

Jennifer's eyes widened. She dropped her voice to a fierce whisper. "I did not cheat!"

"You cheated me out of a true victory." The fact still pissed him off.

"What are you talking about?" She squinted her eyes with incomprehension. "You got the highest score."

"But what good is it if my peers don't take the exam seriously?"

Her sigh shuddered through her. "I did."

"Then why'd you blow off the exam?" He leaned his shoulder against the wall.

"It doesn't matter." Jennifer sat down on the bench. Bryan wondered how she could make something as simple as crossing her legs into something so prissy. "You won, you moved on. Just as I expected you would."

Damn, he knew that stubborn look of hers. He wasn't going to get his answer. It was something that bothered him more than he cared to admit. "So that's it? Giving me a wide berth for top score was my kiss-off? Thanks."

"No," she said as her jaw set with annoyance. "Let's look at it this way. If I had won, you wouldn't have been able to handle it. If I had lost, you would beat your chest,"—she knocked her fists against her sternum—"do a Tarzan yell and move onto the next challenge. I just sped up the process."

Bryan stared at her. He felt like he'd been punched in the gut. She thought he couldn't handle a successful woman? And that he'd dump her ass the moment she wasn't successful enough? "Bull."

Her eyebrow shot up. "You calling me a liar?"

"Yeah, even to your face." It was the least he could do after she described him as the ultimate jerk. "Do you know what I think?"

"I'm breathless with anticipation to find out." Jennifer shifted into a more casual pose. Too casual. "Why did I fail the exam?"

He fought to keep eye contact. He needed to see her reaction. " 'Cause you were scared."

She snorted and rolled her eyes. "I don't get scared. What could I possibly be scared of?"

Steady . . . steady . . . He waited until he got her attention back and ensnared her gaze with his. "Of doing your absolute best and finding out that I was better."

She blinked, but he saw the truth, had his suspicions confirmed, before she looked away. "You're wrong."

"No, I'm not."

She combed her hand through her hair, letting the soft blond tresses drift along her skin. Shielding her face. "I'm not scared of the other guys in Encryption who are a higher level than me."

"You never saw them as your competition. You also hadn't slept with them. Or fallen in love. Lost control. Surrendered everything to them." He felt his breath catch in his throat. He was blowing smoke, saying his hopes out loud and acting like they were fact. He shouldn't have taken such a risk.

Her glare was arctic. "I didn't surrender to you."

It took superhuman strength not to smile. Or collapse with relief. "Almost." She didn't deny the rest. Didn't she notice that? He sure wasn't going to point it out.

"We'll never know, will we?" Jennifer said as she stood up, showing signs that she was getting restless and had enough. "You left immediately for training and I didn't hear from you."

"That's because I was angry." And hurt. Destroyed.

She flashed him a disbelieving look. "At winning?"

"At you," he corrected quietly. "You don't respect me. You might lust after me, might still love me, but you never respected me."

"Bryan, I—"

It was bad enough that she didn't respect him. The last thing he wanted was to hear her say it. "That's all going to change with this wager."

Jennifer pursed her lips. "You're that sure—that delusional—that you're going to win?"

"I know it."

"Oh, did you think that little heart-to-heart was going to soften me up?" she asked as she tried to get by him. "Think again."

"Haven't you been listening? I want you to challenge me. Give me your best shot."

"Bryan, don't worry about that." She reached out and patted him on the cheek. "By the end of this wager, you will be begging for mercy."

He encircled her wrist with his fingers and held her steady before placing his mouth against her open palm. He felt her pulse trip as he pressed his mouth against her warm skin. "Bring it on."

Chapter 4

9?/($$?*-?1/?%@/7~82?&$#%17?>72;?%7

Bryan Matthew went into full alert when he saw Jennifer walking in his direction. It was about time she got here. He didn't like the idea of her strolling around Potomac Park at midnight. He'd thought she would have shown more common sense. Next time he was going to place a curfew on the code.

Settling deeper on Einstein's lap, Bryan found the twelve-foot tall bronze statue icy cold. But he wasn't going to move, not when he had a vantage point and could watch Jennifer undetected.

She wore a dark, straight skirt that went to her ankles. Typically impractical of her, like the flimsy shoes. At least her sweater was doing something to protect her from the cold. It was fluffy and looked soft, but thanks to the lack of light, he couldn't make out the color.

On the other hand, he could tell right off that she looked impatient. Frazzled. The way she stood, the way she kept checking her watch. Definitely a woman on edge.

Bryan folded his hands behind his head. He probably should make his presence known. Then again, what was the fun in that?

And he was having too much fun. Jennifer's latest code nearly melted his brain. It was tough to break and even tougher to figure out the location. But he did it in time. Could Einstein have done better? Okay, bad example, Bryan decided as he looked up at the statue's face.

He'd been living in DC off and on for years and didn't know this Albert Einstein statue existed. It was in a secluded area among a grove of trees. One almost had to be looking for it to see it.

And why did he feel Jennifer betted on that possibility? Trust her to point out that she knew something he didn't—even in code. He couldn't wait to see her expression when she found out that she underestimated him. Again.

He silently watched Jennifer hike up her skirt, exposing her bare legs as she climbed on the statue. It was obvious that she had plans to spy on him, not knowing that he was already there watching her.

She saw him when she reached Einstein's lap. Her shriek could have pierced his eardrum. "Bryan!"

He reached out and grabbed her hand before she tumbled off. "Yeah?"

She punched his leg with her free hand. "You almost gave me a heart attack. What are you doing up here?"

"Waiting for you." He hauled her onto the statue and settled her against him. It was a tight fit, not that Bryan was complaining.

Jennifer pressed her lips together and scooted an inch away. He couldn't tell if she was mad or trying to practice self-restraint. Since this was Jennifer, he was betting she was spitting mad.

"I've been here for a while," Bryan slid closer. "You said you weren't going to rely on numbers in the code, which turned out to be a lie—"

"I was throwing you off the scent," Jennifer explained with supreme dignity.

"But I also figured you'd use artwork again. It was simply a matter of deduction."

"Oh." She leaned away, keeping her distance.

"Fortunately, I knew that what you gave me were Einstein's mathematical equations of the photoelectric effect, the theory of general relativity and the equivalence of energy and matter." Bryan pointed to Einstein's left hand that held a paper showing the three equations.

"And you can pronounce them, too. I'm so impressed."

"I knew you wouldn't use the Albert Einstein Planetarium. That was too obvious. It had to be something that most people wouldn't know about."

"You can stop gloating anytime."

"Your mistake didn't slow me down, either."

Jennifer froze. "What mistake?"

"Come on!" He pulled the deciphered code from his black jeans. "You switched two elements in the photoelectric effect."

"Let me see that." She snatched the paper from his fingers.

"Don't even think about destroying the evidence," Bryan warned, hooking his arm around her shoulders. "We both know you tried to throw me off."

Jennifer glared pointedly at his hand and grabbed his fingers resting on her sweater. "The only thing I'm going to throw you off of is this statue," she replied as he removed his arm from her shoulders.

"Doesn't change the fact that you gave me the wrong equation."

"A lot of good that did," she muttered.

"So you admit it!" he proclaimed in a tone that would make any lawyer on TV proud.

"Admit what?"

"Either you made a mistake and own up to it." He knew deep in his bones it was an honest error, but he would take any chance to tease her. Torment her. Have all of her attention on him. "Or you tried to trick me and showed bad sportsmanship."

Jennifer raised her eyes heavenwards and clucked her tongue. "I admit nothing."

"Of course you wouldn't," he said as he snatched the paper from her hand and stuffed it in his jeans pocket. "Because either way, I'm the better codebreaker."

"Either way, you're not getting a sixty-nine from me."

Hmm. Bryan wagged his eyebrows in interest. Why was she thinking of the deal if she was accused of bad sportsmanship? "Now who has sex on the brain?"

"Oh, shut up."

"But while I'm thinking about it," Bryan tapped his finger against his cold lips, "I should get some sort of consolation prize for my trouble."

"So now I'm a prize?"

Bryan snorted at the thought. "Believe me, babe, that you ain't. You almost cost me the game."

She was unmoved by his argument. "I thought the mistake didn't slow you down," she pointed out, "so how did that almost cost you?"

"A lesser codebreaker would have stumbled," he said as righteously as he could, not that he knew the first step in how to act virtuous. "I think I deserve a kiss."

Her head jerked. "A kiss is reserved for winners." She slowly backed up, ready to take flight.

Before she could move, Bryan blocked her with his arm. "I'm going to win anyway."

Jennifer pushed at his shoulders but he wasn't going anywhere anytime soon. She growled with frustration. "You are so full of yourself."

His mouth was against her ear. "Kiss me, Jennifer."

"Why should I?" She turned her head to the side. "That's like admitting early defeat."

CODE PINK / 127

"Kiss me because you want to," he suggested as he caught her earlobe between his teeth.

"In that case you will be waiting for a very long time." She winced as he bit down.

"I promise I won't kiss back." Much.

"So the point of the entire exercise is?" Her breath hitched as he trailed his mouth along her jaw.

"You control the kiss." The idea had merit. Of being claimed by her. Heat swirled and rippled in his groin. He couldn't wait to bury himself in her warmth.

"You make me sound like a control freak," she complained in a husky voice.

"That's because you are."

She turned, her glare hot enough to smite him. "And you sound desperate for a kiss."

"I am. For your kiss."

She reared back. "Why do you want me to kiss you?"

"Because then you're not talking," he said as he captured her mouth with his.

Anticipation boomed against Jennifer's breastbone as Bryan lowered his head. She forgot to breathe as he pressed his mouth against hers. His heat softened her cold lips, igniting her hunger.

She inhaled his scent as she deepened the kiss. The need flared and licked her blood. Jennifer wanted more. More of Bryan. She needed to taste him and remember.

Cupping her hands against his lean face, she murmured as his shadowed chin scratched her palms. She wanted to feel the bite of his rough whiskers all over her skin.

But Bryan apparently had different ideas. He continued to savor her mouth, sampling her at his leisure, starting from one corner of her lips and making a slow journey to the other edge.

She didn't want teasing kisses. She wanted his lips on her, hard and fast, taking her breath away along with every thought in her head. She wanted to be consumed whole.

Bryan drew back a fraction as her kisses grew frantic. "Jennifer," he said in a groan, bunching her sweater in his fists. "We can't do this here."

"Why not?" She wanted him. Here. Now. This very moment. She couldn't stop. She didn't want to.

Bryan clamped his hands down her waist, his fingertips biting into her flesh. "Your timing sucks," he said against her mouth.

"Who cares?" She slipped her hands under his sweater. His hiss reverberated in her as she palmed his hot skin.

"I know what you're doing."

"I should hope so," she said as she raked her nails against his nipples. "It hasn't been that long for you, has it?"

"You're avoiding a confession," he accused as she hitched his gray sweater up, revealing the hard, sculpted muscles.

Her eyes widened. Maybe the shadows were playing tricks, but his abs were more defined since she last saw him. They were drool-worthy to begin with, but now she couldn't stop exploring every dip and swell.

"And while I applaud your methods," he continued hoarsely, "I'm not falling for it."

"Glad to hear it." She dipped her head and pressed her tongue against his hard nipple. He tasted of hot male and she was suddenly insatiable.

"Tell me the truth." The words barely made it past his throat. "Was it a mistake—the Einstein quote—or did you do it on purpose?"

She bit down, smiling as his tension rippled under his skin. Her nipples stung as they furled in response. Her breasts felt heavy and full.

"Jennifer," Bryan said in a harsh whisper, his hands flexing in her hair.

"Do you want me to stop?" she asked, sliding her fingers down his belly. Need, hot and tingly, spiraled in her own stomach. "Do you *really* want me to stop?"

His fingers tangled in her hair and he yanked her head back. Her heart skipped a beat when she saw the feral lust glittering in his eyes. "Go any farther," he said with soft menace, "and you're in trouble."

She met his gaze evenly as she unbuttoned and slowly unzipped his jeans. The rasp of metal echoed around them.

Bryan's nose flared. "You've been warned."

"And I'm prepared to accept the consequences," she replied as she cupped his penis through his white briefs. "But I didn't realize the consequences would be so . . . hard." He was thick, stiff and hot. Jennifer felt the dampness between her legs as she stroked his length.

Bryan suddenly made his move. He hauled her over until she straddled him, her knees resting on the cold bronze. She blinked dazedly into his eyes, unable to believe that he snatched her so easily—and the power she wielded over him.

Jennifer was keenly aware of the differences between his sleek muscles against her softness. She was ready to surrender and melt into him as he shoved her skirt up to her bottom. Bryan stilled, the tension arcing through him as his hands brushed against nothing but skin.

Usually she wore some frothy scrap of lingerie, but tonight she had nothing under her skirt and sweater. Jennifer had to wonder why she made that decision earlier when she threw on her clothes to meet the deadline. Was it hopefulness of self-fulfilling prophecy?

She shivered as the cold air wafted over her. Goosebumps skittered across her skin. The way he looked at her made her feel beautiful. Desirable. It excited her. Scared her.

"What are you waiting for?" Nervousness made her voice husky. "A written invitation?"

"No." His hands trailed up her stomach. "I'm waiting for you to admit the real reason you're seducing me."

"Isn't it obvious?" she asked, trying not to pant as he splayed his hands on her breasts. At least, not pant loudly. "I want you."

"You want to distract me." He touched her nipples almost reverently. It made her want to weep with frustration.

She clutched his shoulders and arched back. "No, I want you," she argued. And if she didn't have him soon, she would go insane.

"Tell me the truth." He plucked and squeezed her nipples. She felt it all the way to her womb.

"I want you inside me." That was the honest-to-God truth. She could take a lie detector test on it and pass.

"Like this?" he asked. She whimpered when his hands fell away from her breasts. The sound dissolved on her tongue as his fingers speared through her wet curls.

Bryan pressed the tips of his fingers against the entrance of her core. She bucked fiercely but he withdrew. "Tease," she said through gritted teeth. She would get him for this. Make him beg for mercy. Torment him to an inch of his sanity.

"Tell me," he ordered as he held her bare hips.

Her nails dug deeper into his shoulders. "I want you," she said through gritted teeth.

"Yeah, you want me to stop asking for a confession," he added, pressing the rounded tip of his penis into her. And stopped. "So take your time. I can wait."

"Bryan!" She tried to sink down on him, but his hands restrained her.

"Tell me now," he said, his voice shimmering with barely leashed wildness, "or you get nothing more of me."

Jennifer narrowed her eyes. No way. He couldn't. She

ached for him so much that if he left now, the throbbing would haunt her. "You wouldn't."

"Oh, yes, I would. It'll kill me, but I'll do it."

He was bluffing. He had to be. "I don't believe you." She sounded more certain than she felt.

The determination never wavered in his eyes. "On the count of three, Jennifer. One."

She tightened her legs against his. Her wet slit rubbed against his thick erection and she trembled. It felt so good. She moved under him again. And again.

Bryan squeezed his eyes shut as he wrestled for self-control. "Two."

She hooked her arms around his shoulders and pressed her hands against the back of his head. Jennifer was ready to call his bluff. Ready to take him on. She wouldn't let him leave her until she was well and truly satisfied.

"Three."

She slammed her mouth against his, drawing from his strength and took it as her own. Kissing him with every ounce of passion she felt, Jennifer demanded his complete surrender with a fierceness that even startled her.

Bryan's moan vibrated deep in his chest as she rocked her pelvis against his groin. Desire overwhelmed her. Her muscles trembled, desperate for completion.

Jennifer invaded his mouth. With every dip and swirl of her tongue, she diminished his self-control little by little. A heady sense of power pulsed through her.

But she knew that the power had a double edge. As she tried to make Bryan weak with lust, she was seduced by the moment. Her need matched his. Probably more so.

Sweeping her hands along his shoulders and back, she delighted in every shudder she felt under her palm. In a few more minutes she would get everything she wanted and relinquish nothing.

Bryan slowly pulled his mouth away from her. "No

more," he said and firmly lifted her hips away from him, "until you admit why you really want me."

His audacity nearly took her breath away. "Damn it, Bryan!" she yelled, her voice rippling through the cold night air.

"What?" he mocked as he angled her legs apart, leaving her defenseless. "You thought you were winning? Don't mess with the master, Jennifer. I let you get caught in your own web. Now tell me."

She whimpered as tears of frustration welled in her eyes. "There's nothing to tell." She struggled to get the words out. "Now stop stalling."

He neither advanced nor retreated. "Come on, babe," he said in an encouraging tone as his fingers drew tiny circles on her inner thigh. It drove her wild, just as he planned. "Tell me."

Jennifer moved her head from side to side, wishing he would move his finger just a little more to the center. She had to be careful. She might tell him too much. Like how much she still loved him.

"I want you," she confessed weakly. "A lot."

Bryan lowered her, his penis nudging against her core. Teasing. Promising. "And?"

And? She was shaking with need. Couldn't he tell? Wasn't that enough? She looked into his eyes, unable to look away. Jennifer licked her swollen lips that still tingled from his kiss. "So much I can't stand it."

Bryan's expression froze. Oh, God, what did he see? His skin tightened across his features as he groaned. In surrender or triumph?

"Me, too, Jennifer." Bryan whispered brokenly as his hands slid along her back, holding her closer. Holding her tight. He shrouded her, created a cocoon from the world. He was her everything. She couldn't see, hear or touch anything but him. Every scent and taste would be of Bryan.

"Then take me." She closed her eyes, surrendering to the inevitable. Welcoming it. Her breath hitched her throat as he penetrated her. Her flesh gripped Bryan like a hot fist as her knees slid against the icy statue of Einstein.

Bryan held her steady as he slowly pumped into her. It had been so, so long since she made love. Jennifer felt her body ignite into clouds of fires, rolling into each other before spreading out and consuming the edges.

The first orgasmic wave gave an unexpected kick. She pitched forward, colliding into Bryan, gasping for air. Starbursts showered inside her as a white streak flashed across her mind.

The cold bronze bruised her skin as Bryan's thrusts grew harder. Faster. Deeper. Jennifer rode him, propelled by a quest she didn't know she was on. An unreachable dream, perhaps, but at the same time, it offered limitless pleasure. The promise of more spurred her on.

Her heart pounded, her muscles burned. The surroundings blurred and circled her. Tighter, faster, until the atmosphere crackled.

Bryan let out an earthy, masculine yell. His violent release triggered her next climax. She arched back and saw the iridescent colors wash over her. The awe-inspiring beauty humbled her.

Jennifer curled against Bryan, every muscle shaking. She was burning up. Her skin hurt. Her lungs ached, but she managed a small smile.

Their mingled harsh breathing punctured the silence. The quietness gnawed at her. She didn't know why she was compelled to say anything, especially after the way he teased her. "Bryan," she said softly.

"Yeah?"

He sounded out of breath. Worn out. Jennifer's smile widened. Good. "The code for tonight . . ."

She felt him tense underneath her. "Yeah?"

Why wasn't she shutting up? She didn't have to do this. Or did she? Jennifer took a wobbly breath before forging on. "It was a mistake."

"Yeah," Bryan said matter-of-factly, smoothing his hand over her tangled hair. "I know."

Chapter 5

Everything was going to plan, Bryan decided as he headed towards his boss's office the next morning. He was going to win his wager with Jennifer, win her respect, and, if last night was any sign to go by, win her back. About time, too.

He knocked on the door of his superior's office. "Come in," Margaret Mary barked out in her distinctively scratchy voice.

Bryan opened the door and saw the tiny, wrinkled woman behind her huge desk. Her crotchety old lady appearance was deceiving. The woman cussed like an ex-con, could drink all of her agents under the table, and had a black hole where her heart should be. It was no wonder he had a soft spot for her.

"Hi, boss," Bryan said as he strode in, smiling at the older woman. He froze when he saw Jennifer sitting in one of the chairs.

Dressed in a boxy navy blue jacket, pleated skirt and flat shoes, she looked demure. He took in the smooth blond hair, the high collar of her striped shirt, and hell, she'd even gone for the string of pearls. Jennifer Clark looked nothing like he remembered from last night. He found the ladylike image a challenge. How long would it take him to muss her up?

"Yeah, yeah, yeah," Margaret Mary said without looking up from her paperwork. "Sit down."

"What's up?" Bryan asked, lowering himself into one of the empty seats. He shot a questioning look at Jennifer, but she shrugged in response.

Margaret Mary was taking her own sweet time in answering. Bryan looked at his boss who was scrawling her signature on a piece of paper. He could hear the pen digging deep and wondered if it gouged the desk underneath.

"This week," Margaret Mary said, preoccupied with another sheet of paper, "Jennifer put in her paperwork for a new assignment."

Bryan swerved his head so fast that he felt something in his neck pop. Jennifer kept her attention on their boss, but he saw the defiant tilt of her chin. Now if only he could see what kind of game she was playing. "This *week*?" he repeated.

Margaret Mary looked up from her paperwork and glared at him. Glaring for what reason, he wasn't sure. Interrupting. Breathing. The possible list was endless.

"And," his boss enunciated, "she's qualified for the same assignment you're up for."

This didn't sound good. His lungs squeezed. Ow. Ow. Bryan frowned and tried to rub the ache away.

"Since there's only one opening and two qualified agents . . ."

Uh-oh. His chest tightened and Bryan tried to breathe, but it was hard to do when suffering from a bad case of déjà vu.

"The best way to handle this is with an exam," Margaret Mary decided.

This isn't happening. Bryan closed his eyes. Forget breathing. It was overrated, anyway.

"What's the exam?" Jennifer asked.

He winced at Jennifer's clipped tone. She didn't sound at all like last night. She sounded angry. Furious.

"There's no standardized version for this level," Margaret Mary informed her. "And I'm not going to wait until Human Resources gets off their asses to make one."

"What are you going to do?" Bryan asked as he slowly opened his eyes. "Flip a coin?"

"Nope." Margaret Mary pointed a gnarled finger at him. "You're encrypting a message and it will go to Clark." She tilted her head in Jennifer's direction. "Clark encrypts a message and it'll go to you. Whoever breaks the code first wins the assignment."

Oh, shit. Bryan didn't need to glance at Jennifer. Her anger rippled to him from across the room.

Margaret Mary's eyebrow pointed up. "Got a problem with that?"

He knew the question was rhetorical. "No."

His boss gave a curt nod. "Yeah, that's what I thought. Get to it, guys." She slapped her bony hand on the desk. Bryan was surprised it didn't shatter from the impact. "I'll be at your offices by five o'clock today to pick up your codes."

Bryan rose from his seat as Jennifer bolted for the door. He had to get to her, but she moved faster than he anticipated. By the time he slammed the door behind him, Jennifer had turned the corner. He ran after her, dodging people in the crowded corridor.

"Jennifer, wait!"

She walked as fast as her skirt would allow. "Go away, Bryan."

"No." Did she really expect him to listen? To do as she said?

She turned around and Bryan took a step back. Her eyes glittered, her face was flushed, and she looked amazing. Alive. Not that he was going to tell her that she looked beautiful when she was angry. He knew better.

"You know what?" she asked, glaring at him. "I should have looked deeper with your offer of a wager. I should have known it was about more than proving who was the best."

"You don't think—"

"Oh, come on." She planted her fists on her hips. "This was all a set-up. You did this to familiarize yourself with my style."

"I did what?" He looked around at the other agents milling around them and lowered his voice. "Babe, I don't need that kind of inside information."

She tossed her hands up. "I didn't even see it coming."

"I didn't see it coming, either. I didn't know you put in for a new assignment. Correct me if I'm wrong—and I know you will—but wasn't that the whole point of the wager? If you lost, you would stop wasting away at your present job?"

"I wasn't going to lose," she announced, "and if I chose to get a different assignment, it had nothing to do with you."

"Bull!" It had everything to do with him.

"Go away, Bryan," Jennifer said as she turned her back on him. "I have work to do."

Dread, thick and burning, wrapped around his chest. "What about the test?"

"Don't worry about that," she called out as she headed for her office. "I'm not going to let you get your way that easily."

Good, Bryan decided, taking in a shaky breath. For a second there, it was touch and go. But all was not lost.

. . . so that's basically my life in a nutshell. I'm in yet another competition with Bryan. I don't want him as my adversary. I want him as a partner. A husband. Backup. You can't imagine how difficult it is when the love of your life has the power to totally SCREW you. Be the biggest obstacle to your dreams. And did I tell you that he had the audacity—the gall!—to say that I'm afraid of "surrendering" to him. Well, yeah, wouldn't you?

She hit Send and hoped her sorority sisters Amy and Caroline had some answers to her emergency e-mail. And fast. 'Cause she was pretty much at the point of losing it.

Jennifer stared at the screen, knowing she wasn't going to be the best codebreaker anymore. She wasn't going to be able to win this test. Her skills were obsolete. She'd be stuck in this mundane job until retirement.

And worst of all, she wouldn't have Bryan. She wouldn't have him as a lover, a competitor, not even as the bane of her existence. Okay, maybe he wouldn't dump her when he got the assignment, but it wasn't exactly like he was in love with her. Once this test was over, what would keep him with her? Nothing, that's what.

A message from Caroline appeared in her e-mail account. Jennifer jumped on it as if it were a life preserver. Disappointment hit when she saw it was an Out of Office reply.

It was official, Jennifer decided as she flopped back in her seat. She was going to shrivel and wither away, bored out of her mind.

Well, she wasn't going to take it lying down, Jennifer decided. She was going to ace this test, win the dream assignment and bring Bryan to his knees.

Now all she had to do was get up from her desk and do exactly that.

Any minute now . . .

She looked at the copy of the sent message, wondering how she was going to ace the test. It was obvious that she had to do something different.

Surprising . . .

Daring . . .

Risky . . .

She had nothing.

Jennifer sighed and rubbed the heels of her hands against her eyes. The inside of her eyelids suddenly acted like a movie screen and she could see the words *I want him as a partner. A husband. Backup.* fall like autumn leaves.

Oh, great. Jennifer dragged her hands down her face and opened her eyes. Now she was going crazy to top everything off. How fitting.

The words settled and scattered into a random design. The letters morphed into numbers. And the numbers showed a new way of coding.

Jennifer blindly reached for a sheet of paper and pen, too scared to glance away lest the code disappear. Did it only work for this message? Did the "the love of my life" grouping of syllables offer a unique system? Was she grasping at something that wasn't really there?

She wasn't sure, but she had a feeling once she figured it out, she could use it elsewhere. Jennifer felt the buzz of excitement skittering up her spine. If this style of code worked, she would launch it against Bryan.

And he wouldn't know what hit him.

Bryan saw Jennifer at the end of the work day by the soda machines. She had been hiding in her office and she looked like hell.

He leaned up against the machine and blocked her getaway before she could move. "Jennifer, listen to me."

Her shoulders sagged with weariness. "Get lost, Bryan," she said as she fed the soda machine with coins.

"No. Not until you believe that I didn't plan this. I didn't know Margaret Mary was going to have this kind of exam. How could I? I didn't even know you put in for a new assignment."

Jennifer looked at him for a moment and nodded her head. "You're right."

That was easy. His eyes narrowed with suspicion. Too easy. "You're agreeing so I'll get lost."

"No, I obviously was giving your brain way too much credit," she replied as she pushed a button. "Your mind—Machiavellian as it is—couldn't possibly have predicted these turn of events."

He frowned as he put her explanation on mental rewind. "There's an I'm-sorry-I-was-wrong-to-accuse-you somewhere in there. I'm sure of it."

She bent down to retrieve the soda can. "You can get lost now."

"Have you encrypted a message for me yet?"

She froze. Winced. Gritted her teeth. Her fingers tightened against the can. At first Bryan thought she was in pain when realization hit.

"You didn't do it?" he asked in an outraged whisper.

Her expression went blank. "I'll get around to it," Jennifer said, overflowing with bravado.

"It's due at five o'clock." He glanced at his wristwatch. There was no way she could get anything done by now. "What have you been doing all day?"

"I've been busy, all right?"

Bryan leaned against the machine and tilted his head back. He knew the woman had a tendency to forget everything when she was working, but still. If only she could shift some of that legendary focus on him. The thought made him hot.

"Busy doing what?" he asked.

She opened and closed her mouth. "Stuff."

Great. If that didn't snuff out the heat inside him. She still didn't see him as an equal. As someone whose talents were a threat. She was going to rattle off some stupid code and then, when he won, she could say it was because she didn't have time to give the exam her full attention.

"What?" Jennifer asked, bristling with attitude.

"What?"

"Why are you staring at me like that?"

He sighed and looked down his nose at her. "Just wondering where you hide that self-destructive streak of yours. The one that only comes out when you're in competition with me."

She scoffed at the idea. "I do *not* self-destruct."

"Yeah, you do."

Her lips formed into a tight line. "Do not."

"Do, too."

"Not."

"Too."

She held up her hand. "You're talking trash so that you can mess with my mind. I'm not going to let you do that."

"I don't need to do a head job on you. You're doing great on your own."

"I'm going to win this assignment and then we'll see who does the self-destructing. And here's a heads-up: it's going to be you."

He watched her storm off and considered her words. Yeah, she just might be right about that.

Five o'clock . . . five o'clock . . . Five o'clock!

Jennifer paced the tiled floor of the women's restroom. She had to encrypt a message by five? There was no way.

Sure, she could use her new coding system, Jennifer thought as she nibbled on her thumbnail, weighing the pros and cons. It was untested and had no proven level of difficulty, but it would surprise the hell out of Bryan.

But what kind of message was she going to give him? Encrypt a page from the dictionary? No time. Tell him to go jump in a lake? Too easy.

She had to do something. Anything. Jennifer squared back her shoulders and marched out the door. She had no strategy, but that never stopped her before.

Jennifer turned the corner to her office and collided with Margaret Mary. It was like barreling into a bag of bones. "Sorry!" Jennifer apologized as she caught the older woman.

"It's okay," her boss wheezed. "I put Special Agent Matthew's message on your desk."

He had his done already. Her stomach twisted with dread. Of course he did. Damn it. "I'll get you mine—"

"Got it already and gave it to him."

Jennifer, in the midst of coming up with a devious code in thirty seconds or less, obviously missed part of the conversation. "Gave him what?"

The older woman gave her an I-don't-have-time-for-this look. "Your code."

She must have rattled Margaret Mary more than she thought. "My code?"

"Looked like new stuff, Clark," her boss said as she walked away with a slight wobble. "About fucking time you did something ballsy."

She stared with incomprehension as Margaret Mary turned the corner. What code? New stuff?

Jennifer gasped. Not—! Her eyes widened and stung as panic shot through her body. She ran to her office, her high heels scuffing and slipping across the hard floor.

She looked wildly around her orderly desk, vaguely noticing Bryan's complex code. She hunted through the neat piles of paper even though it would have been impossible for it to have found its way there. Finally, she checked under her desk on the off-chance it had fallen.

It wasn't there.

Her Bryan-is-the-love-of-my-life-and-I-want-him-as-my-husband encrypted message wasn't there!

Oh, God, no. Jennifer covered her face with her hands. She was going to be sick.

She had to get it back. No problem. All she had to do

was find the sheet of paper in his unbelievably messy office, destroy it, come up with a new code and plant it on his desk.

And do it before he discovered the switch.

It was never going to work. She fought back the clawing panic. *There was no need to panic. Do not panic.* After all, even if she couldn't make the switch, what were the chances that he could break her code?

She thought about it for a half a second.

"Oh, God!" Jennifer ran out of her office at warp speed.

Chapter 6

"Jennifer?" Bryan stumbled to a halt at his door when he saw her in his office. "What are you doing here?"

She whirled around to face him. "Uh, hi, Bryan." She yelped as her hip caught the edge of his desk. "I was—"

"Did you already break the code?"

"Code?" He looked like he was on full alert. Tense. Ready to pounce. "Oh, *your* code. No."

Bryan's head jerked back. "No?"

She waved the question aside with the sweep of her hand. "I haven't gotten around to it," Jennifer replied blithely as she returned her attention to his desktop.

"I don't understand." He strode into his office until he stood by her side. "Why not?"

She picked up old Styrofoam coffee cups and pitched them into the waste can. "I have other stuff to do." His nearness was making her nervous. Edgy. How could she hunt through his desk with him standing right there?

"What's more important than breaking my code?"

She shrugged. "Stuff." She tossed year-old department newsletters into the trash. Didn't this guy throw anything away? Apparently not.

"Then why are you here? Hold on, what are you doing? Why are you getting into my desk?"

"I'm always running out of paperclips." She thumbed through a sheaf of papers. "Do you have any?"

"Does my desk look like the supply cabinet?" Bryan asked, his voice was rough with exasperation.

She wrinkled her nose. "Looks like an explosion."

He paused as she felt the tension crackling through him. "You're looking for something."

"Paperclips. You know"—she pressed her thumbs against her index fingers—"the metal things that clip paper together. Hence the name."

He pointed an accusing finger at her. "You're looking for clues to break my code."

"What?" Shocked, she stopped rifling through a tower of books and looked at him.

"Clues," he repeated, drawing the word out. "You know, a guide or a hint to solve a problem. Hence the name," he mimicked.

"Thanks for the definition, professor," she said as she opened up the middle drawer, scanned through the contents and slammed it shut, "but I don't need to break into your office to find that."

"Then why did you break into my office?"

She wanted to wipe that smug look off his face. "Paper. Clips."

His gray eyes lit up with unholy glee. "So you did break in. Fess up, Jennifer. You can't break my code."

She slammed a clipboard on the desk, turned and glared at him. "You are so off the mark."

"You can't break the code," he said, ticking off with his fingers what promised to be a long list. "You can't admit to it, you can't tell me that you're cheating—"

"I am not cheating!"

"Looks like it to me." Bryan leaned up against his desk and folded his arms across his chest. "If you're not cheating, what are you doing?"

Jennifer pressed her mouth in a straight line. She didn't want to tell him, but he was obviously jumping to worse conclusions. "I'm looking for my code," she mumbled reluctantly.

"Huh?"

She took a deep breath and looked him in the eye. "I need my code back."

Bryan reached into his back jeans pocket and pulled out a folded white paper. "You mean this?"

Her heart pounded in her ears. "That's it!" She tried to snatch the code, but Bryan held the paper out of reach.

"Unh, unh, unh. Tell me why you need it back first."

Damn. Jennifer curled her fingers into fists. Of course he wouldn't hand it over. That would be way too easy. "Uh, Margaret Mary picked up a . . . highly sensitive document by mistake."

His forehead crinkled as he frowned. "That you encrypted?"

"Yeah."

He shrugged. "What's the big deal? We're both the same level. We're both classified to see the same stuff."

"No!" She made a grab for the paper but held back at the last moment. "I mean, no, this is different."

He held the paper up higher. "How is it different?"

"I'm not . . . authorized,"—*yeah, that's a good one*—"to tell you."

"Right." It was obvious he didn't believe a word she said. "How much do you want this back?"

"You have to give it back to me." Even if it meant wrestling him to the ground for it. Come to think of it, she wasn't above crawling up his body to get the code.

His eyebrow arched. "How badly?" he asked with a dangerous glint in his eyes.

"How badly do you want a sixty-nine?"

His eyebrows shot to his hairline. "That much?" He glanced up at the paper. "I think I'll hang on to it."

That's it. "Give it to me!" She grabbed his arm and tried to hoist herself closer to the code.

"Whoa! Whoa!" He shook her off and her feet landed on the floor with a clatter. "I don't think so."

"I'll give you another code," she promised sweetly.

He paused and considered the option. "Hmm. No."

"Why not?" Her complaint sounded more like a growl.

"It's not that I don't trust you—no, wait. That is the reason. I don't trust you."

"Come on, Bryan. I can't let you break that code."

"Yeah, because then that would make me the winner."

"No, I can't let you break *that* code."

"This code." The paper twitched mockingly in his hand.

"Yeah, that one."

"Hold on." The teasing glint in his eyes disappeared in an instant. His intense gaze unnerved her. "Hold everything. You're scared that I'm going to break this."

"I wouldn't say scared," Jennifer said as she brushed the hair from her eyes. "I don't get scared."

"You think I can break this," Bryan said with a smile. "Without any help. Without cheating."

Oh, great. It has come to this. "Yes."

"On time." His smile widened. "And win."

If he started to gloat, she would not be held responsible for her actions. "Yes, already."

"Okay." He lowered his arm and offered her the code. "Here you go."

His full-wattage smile dazzled her. Jennifer blinked. Blinked again. "You're giving it to me?" She reached for the paper and pulled back as if she was afraid she would get burned. "What's the catch?"

"No catch."

She grabbed the paper from his hand before he thought of one. "You're not getting the sixty-nine because of it," she reminded him as she crumpled the code in her hand. "You passed on that particular deal."

"I know," he said with exaggerated regret. "Give me another code before you start working on mine."

"That's it?" Something wasn't right here.

"That's it."

It was too good to be true. She studied his expression, but she saw no danger lurking. "Why?"

" 'Cause I got what I wanted. Your respect."

Guilt bloomed inside her. All this time she could have said something, but she refused to. Because she saw it as the one thing that protected her. How stupid could she be? She had a long way to go to make up for her pettiness. "You always had it," she admitted quietly.

"You had a strange way of showing it," Bryan said as he cupped her elbow and escorted to the door. "And you would rather go through enemy torture than admit it."

"True." She looked down at the wrinkled code in her hand. Was she making the same mistake? Did she think by not telling him how she felt, she was protecting herself?

There was only one way to find out. If she got hurt, then she had no one to blame but herself. But she had to take a risk with the belief that this was the best move.

"Here," she held up the paper, hating how her hands trembled, "you can have it back."

Bryan looked doubtfully at her. He slowly retrieved it from her tight grasp. "Are you sure?"

"Yeah, I'm sure." Not really. She stared at the paper, the fierce pounding of her heart hurting her ribs.

Anyway, she wasn't one to get scared, right? Oh, who was she kidding? Maybe she never felt the bone-deep fear that she was experiencing right now because she never took a chance. Not on something that mattered this much.

"So I guess we're settled," Jennifer said, dragging her eyes away from the one thing that was going to break apart her safe and secured cocoon. Maybe if she broke his code fast enough, he wouldn't finish breaking hers. "We don't need to do the third code of our wager."

"I didn't say that."

She stomped her foot. "Come on, Bryan," she whined. "I have work to do."

"Nope. I'm on a roll. Today you admit I'm good," he said as he slowly closed the door between them. "By tomorrow, you'll admit that I'm the best."

Chapter 7

?7?2>7%$?8~/@?1-*?(?%?;<$?28

"Come on . . . come on." Bryan muttered as he watched the floor numbers drag by. The moment the elevator doors opened, he burst onto the floor.

This wasn't happening, he thought as he searched like mad for the right room. The pounding of his feet on the carpet matched with his thudding heartbeat. *He couldn't be late. Not this time.*

Bryan passed the room and backtracked. He glanced at his watch and could feel the cold sweat break out on his forehead. The deadline was too close for comfort.

He slipped the card key in the lock. The red light glared at him, barring entry. "Damn!" he said under his breath. He swiped it again with a shaky hand. Bryan let out a sigh of relief when he saw the green light and wasted no time in throwing the door open.

Darkness greeted him. The room was still and silent. Disappointment crashed through Bryan. His shoulders dipped in defeat just as Jennifer's voice wafted on the other side of the room.

"You made it. Barely."

Something wasn't right, he decided as he brushed his

hands along the wall, looking for the light switch. Jennifer didn't sound pissed. More like . . . pleased? Wait, that couldn't be right. What was going on?

He hit the lights and found her in the large bed. She appeared naked under the sheets, but that might be wishful thinking on his part. Now was not the time to jump to any conclusions. He was not going to take a flying leap into bed. Not yet, at least. "Did you break my code?" he asked as he squeezed the door handle, the metal biting into his skin. "For the test?"

"Yep. Hours ago."

Hours? He would have heard something about it by now. She was bluffing.

"You did not."

Jennifer rested her chin on her knees, the bed sheets offering tantalizing glimpses of skin and curves. "Your message said that you loved me and that I would always come first in your life," she quoted and ended with a sigh.

Bryan grimaced. He had bared his heart in that code, but he didn't remember it sounding that sappy. Jennifer looked kind of teary-eyed, so maybe it wasn't so bad. "It looks better on paper."

"I liked it," she declared. "I might even frame it. Embroider it on a pillow."

"Don't even think about it," Bryan ordered as he kicked the door closed and tossed the card key on a nearby table. "Why didn't you call it in with Margaret Mary?"

She shrugged. "I'll get around to it. I have more important stuff to do. So," she added oh-so-casually, "did you break *both* my codes?"

"Yeah."

Jennifer nibbled her bottom lip. "Hard, huh?"

She sounded breathless. Nervous.

"Very."

"Glad you made it," she said softly.

"Why are you?" He shrugged off his coat. "It means I won our wager."

"Yeah, I know." She didn't sound peeved about it.

He tossed his coat on the floor and strode towards the bed. The call of the hunt pounded through his blood. This time, he wasn't going to ignore it. "And I don't remember the code saying anything about getting naked."

"Clothing is optional." She darted her tongue across her bottom lip.

He shucked off his shoes. "Apparently."

"Aren't you going to say anything?" Annoyance edged her words.

Bryan grabbed the neckline of his sweater and pulled. "About what?" His voice was muffled underneath the sweater.

"My code."

His sweater sailed across the room. His skin felt hot and tight already. He couldn't get naked fast enough for his liking. "Yeah."

She waited tensely for a second. "And?"

"Watergate?" he complained as he stripped off his jeans and underwear. "Of all the places we could meet in DC, you picked the Watergate Hotel?"

Jennifer frowned. "What's wrong with it?"

"I sense there's some sort of hidden message there." The rest of his clothes followed his sweater and he crawled onto the bed.

She rolled her eyes. "No hidden message. I swear."

He grabbed the edge of the sheets and yanked them from her. It was like unwrapping a much anticipated present. He stopped and stared at her, his eyes greedily taking in her pale skin and soft curves.

"Bryan!"

"What?" he asked innocently.

She grabbed the sheets and held them against her. "The other message," she reminded him as her nostrils flared.

"Oh." Bryan straddled her legs and leaned into Jennifer, watching her slowly recline onto the mattress. "The one about you still loving me and wanting to have my babies."

Jennifer froze. Her mouth dropped open with surprise and her eyes bugged out. "I most certainly did not say anything about babies!"

"It was inferred." He rested his forearms on either side of her head. "Don't you want kids?"

"I want you to tell me how you feel first," she answered through clenched teeth.

"About what?" Having Jennifer underneath him was causing havoc on his senses. It felt too good.

She tapped his shoulders with her fists. "My code, you moron!"

"Hey." He grabbed her wrists and held her hands above her head. "That's no way to talk to the love of your life."

She squeezed her eyes shut and shook her head. "I'm never going to live that down, am I?"

"Probably not." He lowered his mouth on her cheek and brushed feathery kisses down her jaw line. The way she shivered with delight made his cock stir more.

"I should have taken the code back while I had the chance," she said in a grumble, her eyes opening halfway.

He paused, the idea darkening his mood. "No way. You would never have told me otherwise."

"I would have," she argued, arching her neck as he trailed his mouth down the side of it. "Eventually."

"Yeah, right," he said, his mouth hovering over the pulse point at the base of her throat. "When I got old and had one foot in the grave."

He felt her tense swallow under his mouth. "But I meant what I said," she said in a husky tone. "I don't want you as an adversary. I want you as backup."

Bryan raised his head and looked directly into her eyes. "And as a husband," he added in a satisfied growl.

Her cheeks turned pink. She pulled against his hands, but he didn't let go of her wrists. Jennifer looked away, stopped herself, and returned her gaze to him. "Yeah."

"So . . ." Bryan felt the adrenaline rushing through him as if he was on the top of a rollercoaster and ready to take the plunge. He wasn't concerned about the dangers or about getting hurt. He was worried that he wouldn't catch every minute of the wildest ride of his life. "When *are* you going to marry me?"

Jennifer's breath hitched in her throat. Marry. Her throat hurt, but she was afraid to exhale. Afraid to lose this moment. She wanted to be with Bryan so much. Wanted him to be her partner in the home, in bed and in her life.

Jennifer kissed him hard. She felt the joy inside her ready to burst from her skin. She wrapped her legs around his and thrust her hips against him, needing to show him how she felt, needing him to share it.

Bryan let go of her wrists and cupped her face with possessive fingers. "I take it that means soon?"

Her hands immediately pulled his head closer to hers. "Your cryptanalysis prowess is amazing," Jennifer said against his mouth before she deepened the kiss.

Her nerve endings lit like a row of lights as Bryan's hands caressed her body. He made her feel alive. Jennifer had missed this intimacy she had shared with him.

She never wanted it to end. She explored his body with her hands and mouth with growing insistence. Jennifer knew just how to commemorate the renewal of their relationship. A sensual celebration.

Sitting up, she rolled Bryan to the side. Jennifer ignored his protests and grasping hands as she reversed her position. She felt the tension in Bryan as she lay down with her head at level with his hips.

"Jennifer?" Cautious excitement lurked under the question. "What—"

She grasped his penis in her hands. He felt hot and smooth under her touch. "Don't you want to claim your prize?"

"Did you cheat on something I should know about?" Bryan asked gruffly.

She chuckled. "No, I'm talking about the first offer of a sixty-nine, that one you stole." She lapped the rounded head with the tip of her tongue, tasting him. "From Robert," she reminded him.

His body pitched forward in response to the promise. Bryan stiffened and held himself in check. "Don't talk about another guy while you're doing that to me, okay?"

"I'll keep that in mind for future reference."

His self-control suddenly snapped and his hands clasped her bottom. "Doesn't someone need to be on top?" he asked as he squeezed her flesh. "Like you?"

"Where's the spirit of equal partnership in that?" she teased. She roughly fondled his testicles with her other hand. Bryan's staggered groan made her smile.

His fingers were like branded steel against her hips. She flinched as his fingertips dug into her skin when she indulged in the taste of hot, musky male. Jennifer licked and laved the length of his penis, murmuring her pleasure.

He hooked her leg over his head and began an unhurried journey to her wet center. She shivered as his whiskered jaw rasped against her inner thigh. Bryan's hot breath wafting over her sensitive skin added to her delight.

Jennifer surrounded the tip of his penis with her lips. She sucked his slick flesh and Bryan drew back before plunging his tongue into her center. She groaned against him as she felt him deep inside her. Ribbons of pleasure unfurled from her womb and crackled out to the edges of her body.

With one hand clasped against her bottom, Bryan held her close against him. His other hand worked in tandem with his mouth, building the desire inside her to a fever pitch. She writhed against him as the pleasure built low inside to the point of discomfort. She felt like she was going to explode, but it was too soon.

He caressed her clit with his tongue and fingers. Pleasure bubbled inside her as she drew Bryan deeper into her mouth, her lips stretched around him. As she sucked, her teeth grazed the underside of his penis.

Jennifer felt the pleasure forking through her veins like lightning. She released him as she went rigid. "Bryan!" Satisfaction foamed through her and overflowed.

Bryan flipped her on her back. She couldn't object to his high-handedness as he knelt between her legs. While she still rode the waves, Bryan slid into her core. Jennifer arched her spine, accommodating his length.

He began to thrust, each move deep and powerful. The sheets and pillows fell to the floor. She slithered along the length of the mattress with each stroke until her shoulders dipped past the corner.

Jennifer felt Bryan's muscles shuddering with slipping control. She used the last of her strength and wrapped her legs around his waist. He grabbed her shoulders and drove into her one last time.

Her topsy-turvy world shattered into an explosion of color. As Bryan pulsed inside her, she was swept away like a storm of confetti.

When Bryan collapsed on top of her, she gravitated to his solid strength. She clung to their tangle of heat and sweat. Their mingled breaths echoed in her ears.

"Bryan," she croaked out, "you do not understand the basics of equal partnership."

He lifted his head and studied her face. A smile tugged at his reddened lips. "Says who?"

"A partner does not grab all the power—"

"I don't know about that," he argued as he picked her up and brought her back to the head of the bed. "I was feeling a bit weak in the knees for a while there."

"And devour his partner until she's clinging to him for dear life." She gave an exaggerated sigh. "I guess I'll have to show you again."

"Guess so," Bryan said, satisfaction flooding his words. He cradled her back firmly against his chest. He draped his leg over her hip, his hand splayed against her breast. He surrounded her. Kept her warm. Kept her close.

She slowly relaxed in his embrace, unable to grasp the fact that life was good. She won everything she went after. She had Bryan. She aced the test. She got the assignment.

Or did she? Jennifer frowned as a thought niggled in the back of her mind. He never did admit his defeat on that point. "Bryan? You're okay with me getting the assignment, right?"

"Yeah," he said in a sleepy voice against her ear. "As long as you call me champion. Daily. In public."

Jennifer turned to face him. "Uh, two tests do not make you a champion." She felt it was necessary to straighten him out on that score. "What about all those times when I got the top score and you didn't?"

"The results from our wager cancel—"

She flattened her hands against the back of his head and kissed him. A kiss that she felt down to her toes.

"What was that for?" Bryan asked when he needed to come up for air.

"To keep you from talking." She wiggled closer against him. "How chatty are you feeling?"

The gleam in his eye made her tingle. "Very."

Fantasies Are Forever

Chapter 1

"Okay, Mia. It's your turn."

Caroline Mitchell glanced at her friend Mia and braced herself. Being a part of this temporary Dream Circle went way beyond the call of friendship. And although her friend Artemis said one didn't have to be Wiccan to take part in the ritual, Caroline felt particularly witchy after suffering through Mia's retellings of her dreams.

But she wouldn't dare show her discomfort. Caroline propped her elbow on the cafeteria table and placed her chin on her fist. She had to keep a blank expression.

"Well," Mia said as she leaned forward, enthusiasm glowing from her eyes. "It's a slight variation from the one I told you last week. In this one, I had a blindfold."

"You didn't see anything in your dream?" Caroline asked hopefully.

"No, it was like an out-of-body experience. I saw everything—and I mean *everything*. My lover was seriously well-hung." Mia demonstrated with her hands.

Caroline glanced around the crowded cafeteria, but no one seemed to notice Mia's explicit hand gestures. Either the employees at the Seattle-based aromatherapy company were used to Mia or they were too hungry for lunch to care.

"So." Mia leaned farther in until her chin almost touched the table. "I'm buck naked on this guy's bed and I'm so ready for him."

And I'm so not ready to hear this, Caroline thought.

"But he's just teasing me. His hands and mouth are all over me, never staying in one place for long." Her fingers continually moved as she spoke. "Just long enough to have me panting. My nipples are about ready to shoot off like a rocket, you know?"

How much longer until their lunch break was over? Caroline was tempted to check her watch.

"And then, all of a sudden,"—Mia sliced her hand in the air—"nothing."

Caroline raised her eyebrows. "You woke up?" It was too good to be true.

"No, he stops touching me. Completely. I'm shaking, ready to have the mother of all orgasms, and this guy won't even jill me off."

Caroline nibbled the inside of her cheek, wondering when Artemis's regular Circle was going to get back from their hiatus.

"So I reach for my blindfold and I hear this voice." Mia dropped her voice in what Caroline assumed was an attempt to be masculine. " 'Move the blindfold and I will tie your wrists to the bed.' "

It was strange that a Dream Circle would need a break, Caroline decided. Very odd, indeed. Maybe they had dreamers like Mia. Although, she would think nothing fazed a group of witches.

"But he still doesn't touch me. I can't handle the anticipation. I'm squirming all over the bed," Mia said, wiggling in her seat, giving Caroline a visual she would have rather not had, "and I don't feel him next to me. I call out for him, but he doesn't answer. I can't even hear him breathe. I start thinking he might have left me."

"Wait a second," Artemis interrupted. "I thought you were able to see everything due to your out-of-body view."

"But now I'm on a close-up where all I can see is me. So I grab for my blindfold and just as I lift it up, the guy grabs my wrist. And he says, 'I told you not to touch the blindfold.'"

Well, duh. It was like those teen horror films where the ingénue opens the very door everyone tells her not to.

"And before I know it, my hands are tied up." Mia raised her hands above her head and crossed her wrists. "I can't move my arms at all. My blindfold is still on and this shadow descends on me."

The Dream Circle's hiatus is beginning to look suspiciously permanent.

"I know that either I'm going to have the best fuck of my life or,"—Mia lowered her arms—"I'm going to die of frustration."

"So then what happened?" Artemis asked.

Don't encourage her! Caroline flashed Artemis a warning look. She didn't see it, too fascinated by what Mia had to say.

"I don't know. I woke up." Mia shrugged and took a long gulp from her soda can. "So what do you think my dream means?"

Was she serious? Caroline dug her fist into her cheek. She wasn't going to give her opinion. It would only prolong the agony.

"It could mean that you are looking for structure in your life," Artemis said, steepling her fingers as she interpreted the dream. "You're seeking situations that offer set rules and definite consequence."

Caroline rubbed her temples with her fingertips. She wasn't going to comment. Wasn't going to comment . . .

"As for the blindfold, I'm not sure. Let me look it up." Artemis thumbed through her worn dream reference book.

"It could either mean that you are ignoring the need for change, or it's a cry for guidance."

Caroline slapped her palms on the table, unable to take it anymore. "It means," she said, looking straight at Mia, "you need to get some action with a real man, not with the wimps you date."

"Hmm." Mia pursed her lips and tilted her head. "I have to admit, I like Caroline's interpretation better," she told Artemis with regret.

"How many times do I have to explain this?" Artemis asked, exasperation blurring her voice. "Sex could represent many things in a dream. It doesn't necessarily mean that Mia had a sexual fantasy."

"Are you kidding me?" Caroline gestured toward Mia. "That was a classic wet dream. She should submit it to *Penthouse*."

"You think?" Mia was intrigued.

Artemis let out a long-suffering sigh. "Perhaps she's seeking direction in the sexual aspect of her life."

Mia nodded her head at the possibility. "The guys I've been dating lately have been . . ."

"Beta?" Caroline suggested.

"Gentlemen?" Artemis asked.

"Boring," Mia finished.

"Who are you dating?" Caroline asked. It was hard to keep track. The self-proclaimed office slut took her title more seriously than her job description.

"The tech support team."

"Heh." Artemis scoffed. "Well, that explains it. They're all built like alfalfa sprouts. Mia, your dreams are obviously telling you to consider the choices you are making. You need to dwell on that. But now it's Caroline's turn to share her dream."

Caroline froze. Was it her turn already? She hated this part. She would rather hear more about Mia's dream.

"Yeah, Caroline." Mia rested her chin on both fists. Her expression was intense. "What does a woman who has done, seen and had it all dream about?"

"I don't know. No matter how hard I try, I can't seem to remember any of my dreams," Caroline lied. She felt horribly guilty, but it was the only way.

"Again?" Mia's eyes widened. "That is so weird. Maybe you're not dreaming. Maybe you don't have anything left to dream about. Oh, that's a scary thought."

"If I'm dreaming, I forget what it's been about the minute I wake up." *Yeah, she wished.*

Artemis leaned back in her seat and crossed her arms. "I've noticed this has happened since you've come back from that wedding in D.C. Not remembering your dreams for one week I can understand. Two weeks, and it's a bit strange. But after all this time,"—her eyes narrowed—"do you know what I think?"

Busted. Caroline hunched her shoulders. "What?"

"Seeing your sorority sister going through a life change like marriage has brought some stressful questions about your own life."

"Whoa." Caroline waved her hands, warding off any more discussion. "You are way off base, Artemis. Believe me, I don't want to get married. Jennifer's wedding didn't uncover any bridal fantasies."

"I don't know," Mia said. "Every time I'm a bridesmaid, I start getting those urges."

Caroline cast a sideways glance. "Thank goodness they have those groomsmen to take care of you, huh?"

"You said it." Mia high-fived her.

"Getting back to Caroline," Artemis said, briskly changing the subject, "I don't want to alarm you, but if you're not dreaming, you're under too much stress."

Considering she was working overtime developing a new product line—ironically, one to reduce stress, under an insane deadline—and had to work closely with a certain sexy coworker, she would have to agree. "I'll keep that in mind."

"I know you don't believe this will work, but you should keep a notepad and pen by the bed," Artemis said. "Then when you wake up, you can write down fragments of your dream before you forget."

Caroline nodded her head. If she did that, two words would keep appearing: Joe Hatcher. The very idea of him made her tingle. What he did to her in those dreams would make Mia blush.

In real life Joe could make her forget who she was when he just said "hi" to her. When he sat next to her in meetings, she felt like she was going to burst through her too-tight skin. Even an e-mail from him could result in stuttering heartbeats, dry mouth and cold sweats.

She'd thought she had grown out of that phase a long time ago. Caroline clucked her tongue in self-disgust. It was not good. Not for her work, her career, or even her self-preservation.

A movement caught her eye. Caroline stiffened before she instinctively looked away. Her heart fluttered against her rib cage, the blood pounding in her ears, blocking out whatever Artemis was saying.

It was definitely not good that the man of her dreams was walking toward her with the determination of a hunter.

The minute he saw Caroline in the cafeteria, Joe felt like he was being plunged into hot oil. His nerve endings screamed for mercy. His blood sizzled.

Now if only he could get the sexy aromatherapist to feel the same, Joe thought wryly as he strode to her table. He caught her gaze and she looked away fast.

Caroline pressed her fingers at the bridge of her nose. Her fingers stilled and she dropped her hand from her face. Joe remembered she'd done that a few times in the past.

He wasn't sure what it meant. While it would be routine for someone who wore glasses, that was not the case with Caroline. Nothing blocked his view of her hazel eyes.

"Hi, Joe," Artemis greeted him warmly as he stopped at their table. "Did you need something?"

"I know you're on your lunch, but I can't find the weekly reports and Huang is breathing down my neck." He hated intruding, but he hated dealing with the Research and Development VP even more.

"They still haven't shown up?" Artemis rose from her seat. "Let me make a few calls."

Joe focused on the woman although he was fully aware of Caroline. Too aware. "I don't want to interrupt."

"No problem," she replied as she collected her books. "We're finished with our Dream Circle for today."

"Dream Circle?" Working with Artemis was always an educational experience.

"My coven usually has a Dream Circle, but we're taking a break until the Summer Solstice. Mia and Caroline accepted the challenge of sharing and interpreting dreams until then."

"Really?" He gave in to temptation and glanced at Caroline, but she was doing her best to ignore him. He would love to find out her dreams.

He didn't care what they were: a trip to Paris, taking the stage with the Rolling Stones, or even a state-of-the-art office chair. Whatever it was, he would gladly make them come true. "Can I join?"

Caroline's head jerked and their gaze connected. Heat, thick and steamy, billowed between them. The force made him step back.

"Women only," she said hoarsely. She cleared her throat and walked away. "Sorry."

Hmm . . . interesting. "What is this? Second grade?" Joe asked, following her.

She tossed her trash in the bin and brushed her hands

together. "Including a man in a Dream Circle would change the dynamics," she replied, as if she had a wealth of experience with this type of thing.

Joe leaned closer to her, inhaling her scent that made his mouth water. "Then maybe we could form our own circle, Caroline," he murmured. "You can tell me your dreams and I'll tell you mine."

"Caroline says she can't remember any of her dreams," Mia announced at Joe's other side, "but I think she's holding out. She must have some really juicy ones."

Joe saw Caroline's guilty start. When she glared at Mia to knock it off, he had to consider the possibility. Were her dreams too hot to share? *Please let that be.*

Caroline caught him staring. Her mouth opened and closed while she searched for words. "Believe me, that isn't the case. Mia suggested I didn't have anything left to dream about, but that doesn't follow Freud's belief about wish fulfillment being the impetus of dreams. Of course, there is that school of thought that says that dreams are suppressed expressions of our deeper selves. . . ."

Wow. Joe stopped and stared at her. Caroline was amazing when she got in the scientific mode. Her hazel eyes, which always shimmered with intelligence and humor, flared and took hold of him. Caroline's long, black hair rippled as she spoke passionately on the topic. He had no clue what the hell she was saying, but he didn't care.

Joe had to wonder what she would look like in bed. He wanted to create that passion in her. And then have that energy focused back on him. He felt tight and heavy thinking about it.

"Then again, Jung suggested that dreams . . ." She sputtered to a stop. She winced, stuck the tip of her tongue between her teeth and bit down.

If that wasn't the most erotic thing he'd ever seen. He wanted to capture her tongue and suck it into his mouth.

The need was so strong that he didn't know if he could keep it at bay for much longer.

"Look at the time," she said and then looked at her wristwatch. A blush zoomed into her face as she suddenly realized she'd reversed her actions. "Yeah, late. See you around."

Joe shoved his hands in his pockets before he tried to restrain her. What had he done wrong this time? "Is she always like that around you guys?" he asked as she bolted out the door.

"Never," Artemis replied, eyeing him speculatively. "Only when you're around."

Caroline saw the first streaks of sunrise stream through her office window. She yawned and clicked the print icon on her computer screen. She was so tired that she wouldn't mind using the keyboard as a pillow.

"Can't fall asleep," she told herself. The words sounded slurred together. Caroline decided it was time to add more of her special peppermint blend in her diffuser.

It was essential to stay awake. Caroline blinked her eyes open. She had to proofread her report. She had things to do. Most of all, she had to avoid her dreams.

Caroline supported her head with her hand. Dreams. Her dreams were troubling. She was constantly dreaming about Joe. At first it was the occasional naughty fantasy that visited her dreams. Then he slowly took over until he stole the leading role.

Artemis might be totally off the mark when it came to dream interpretation, but she was right on one point. Since her friend Jennifer's wedding, all Caroline ever did was dream about Joe. Dream? Fantasies. Fantasies she didn't even know she had, like the mailroom encounter that in reality would probably give her head-to-toe paper cuts. Fantasies that left her frustrated and aroused. That required her to buy batteries in bulk for her vibrator.

She had tried everything to stop dreaming about Joe. All that was left was actually bedding him. But that would be the worst thing. Because Joe was unlike any other man she knew. He made her feel exposed. He reminded her of what she was—a nerd.

And she swore she would never be like that again. No one would see her as just a brain again. She hated being the girl most likely to win a Nobel Prize, but it didn't hurt as much as being voted the girl least likely to find her name and number on the wall of the men's room.

Of course, nothing was as traumatic as when she had been crowned queen of that college party. Even now, after all these years, her stomach churned at the memory. When she found out later it was a party for guys to bring the ugliest, most pathetic date, something inside her died.

Caroline determinedly shoved the memory away. She had survived and that was all that mattered. Like a phoenix rising from the ashes, she transformed herself from a brainiac into a bombshell.

She thought her brainy tendencies had died all those years ago, but they came back full force the moment Joe turned his attention on her. It was unnerving at how he managed to break down her defenses. It was like he could see past the cosmetics and designer clothes and find the girl she used to be. The girl she refused to become again.

After all, would Joe Hatcher give her a second look if she was still a brainiac? Caroline scoffed at the idea as her eyes drifted shut. Had he seen what she'd looked like in college, Joe would keep his distance.

She suddenly remembered her dorm room with startling clarity. The place was a mess, as usual, with clothes, books, and computer paraphernalia. Posters on the wall of Merchant-Ivory films and Albert Einstein indicated it was her pre-transformation time.

But one thing was different. She certainly didn't remember having Joe Hatcher in her single bed. Not that she'd had a steady stream of frat boys coming into her room. Not even a trickle of male students.

Joe wasn't any college guy. He appeared exactly as he did earlier today, charcoal-gray power suit and all. Lounging on her bed, he rested his arm on his knee. As casual as he appeared, Caroline wasn't fooled. He was like a wildcat that could pounce at any moment.

She strode to the bed with more confidence than she possessed and knelt down on the mattress in front of Joe. Her heart pounded to the beat of Cheap Trick's "I Want You to Want Me" blasting from the radio. Her throat constricted as his hands touched the sides of her face before he gently removed her dark-rimmed eyeglasses.

As he placed them on the messy desk next to her bed, Caroline shucked off her Delta Delta Alpha sweatshirt. Much to her surprise, she wore nothing underneath it. She tossed the sweatshirt onto the floor, her mouth dry and tingling with anticipation. Joe knelt in front of her, the mattress dipping where their knees met.

Cradling her head with his hands, he lowered his mouth onto her. Need pricked and stung her skin as he kissed her. Long, wet kisses that curled more than her toes.

Joe's hands drifted down, leaving a trail of goose bumps. Her breasts felt heavy as he cupped her fullness. Caroline hissed when he brushed his thumbs against her nipples.

Their clothes seemed to melt away and Caroline could feel his heat swirling around her. His bronze skin felt hot under her touch. His scent was warm and masculine.

Caroline smoothed her hands over his sculpted chest. His heart thudded, loud and strong, against her palm. She threaded her fingers through the sprinkling of dark hair and followed the descending arrow past his waist.

Her fingers brushed against his cock and she hesitated before she cradled his length in her hands. Joe was smooth, thick and pulsed under her touch. Her stomach felt jittery as her thighs wobbled.

She stroked his cock and his groan of pleasure vibrated against her lips. Joe whirled her around and pressed her back against his chest. He fondled her breasts with rough hands until even the air stung her nipples.

Leaning her head back on his shoulder, Caroline desperately rooted for his mouth. His lips met hers just as his hand dropped down to her abdomen. She shuddered as Joe's fingers speared through the thatch of damp curls before finding her wet slit.

She wrenched her mouth away from Joe as he rubbed her slick folds. Her legs bracketed his as she clawed his lean hips with her hands. Joe held her tightly against him so that her bottom pillowed his cock.

The position made her feel exposed and vulnerable. But she didn't complain. Her choppy panting echoed in her ears. She was ready for more. She was ready to give him anything and everything.

Joe nudged her and she shot her arms out. Her palms slapped the lumpy mattress and she was on all fours in front of Joe. Her flesh clenched around his length and drew him in deeper as he invaded her.

Bucking against him, she shivered as his cock filled her completely. His hands were all over her while she couldn't touch him. A part of her found it unfair, but she refused to have it any other way.

Caroline moaned as he withdrew, tormenting her until he slid into her core again. She arched and dipped like a stretching cat. Her arms and legs shook as the sensations rolled inside her.

He pinched her nipple at the same time that he caught her clit between his finger and thumb. A sharp climax exploded inside her and she heard her keening cry in the distance. The sensations mushroomed and stormed her. Her joints threatened to disintegrate and crumble.

Joe's hands clamped on her hips and he gave a hard

thrust against her. Caroline scrambled her hands in front of her and grabbed fistfuls of the bedsheets.

He thrust harder and faster. The creaking bedsprings sounded like a piercing siren. Joe's furious rhythm was unpredictable, but each thrust hit her deep.

Another climax ignited deep in her pelvis. It flared to life and grew stronger with every thrust. Caroline's breasts slapped against each other as he rode her hard. The bedsheets slipped off the mattress and Joe's hands were the only thing that held her up.

The overwhelming sensations ripped through her. Her mind shattered as she tumbled down. Tumbled into a sea of cotton, wave after wave.

"Caroline?" Joe's voice made her shiver.

"Mmm?" The aroma of orange tickled her nose as the white sheets turned orange. She was suddenly bouncing around on waves and waves of orange cotton. She grabbed for the sheets, but they turned liquid in her hands. She frowned as she saw the droplets clinging to her skin. Not liquid— orange juice.

"Caroline," Joe said a little louder, "you're late for the breakfast meeting."

Hello! Caroline jackknifed up, her spine slamming against the backrest of her chair. "What?" She blinked her eyes open and looked around her office. Full sunlight flooded the small, cluttered room.

Joe stood before her, fully clothed in an expensive black suit, crisp white shirt and red tie. She saw the quirk at the corner of his mouth, but his green eyes didn't waver as he studied her with a disquieting intensity.

He held a bottle of orange juice and offered it to her. What was he doing here? The lyrics from the *Sesame Street* song, "One of these things doesn't belong," started playing in her head.

She could only hope she wasn't singing it out loud.

Chapter 2

"Here." Joe waved the open bottle of orange juice under Caroline's nose. "You're going to need it."

She took the bottle reluctantly. "That bad, huh?" Her fingers feathered the edges of her mouth.

"Do you often do all-nighters at the office?" Visions of him doing her all night intruded into his thoughts. He might have to start camping out in his office and take advantage of any midnight break.

"Uh, no. Just had to get this report done." She glanced at the screensaver on her computer and quickly moved the mouse.

"The report that was due almost half an hour ago?" He watched her wince. "Don't worry, I covered for you."

"Thanks." She looked at him with deep suspicion as she took a sip. "Why?"

What kind of man did she think he was? Joe leaned against her desk. "It's okay. I'm not going to ask for services rendered."

Caroline choked on her orange juice.

"When I take you to bed, it'll be because you want to, not because you have to."

She was the first to break eye contact. "Don't hold your breath," she muttered.

He shrugged off her quick retort. "Why not? And don't give me that crap about not dating coworkers."

Caroline's face brightened. "I gave up that habit for my New Year's resolution."

He flashed her a knowing look. "Right. Sure you did."

"I have to go." She jumped from her seat. Her chair clattered against the wall behind her. "Wash up and get this report out. Talk to you later, Joe."

Hell. Joe watched her hurry from the room. He clenched his fist until his knuckles whitened. What had he done wrong this time? He'd have to find out fast because he was going to have Caroline naked and willing in his bed by the end of the month or go stark, raving mad.

"Caroline," Artemis said sharply at the Dream Circle a week later, "if you don't lift your head up, you're going to be snorting salad."

Caroline jerked her head back. "Sorry," she mumbled. She hastily covered her mouth as she yawned.

"Didn't you get any sleep over the weekend?" Mia asked as she slurped the last dregs of her soda. "I bet you weren't even able to dream, huh?"

"On the contrary." Caroline pushed her salad to the side. "Every time I dream, I wake up."

Artemis's eyebrows dipped into a concerned frown. "Nightmares?"

"Not exactly." She covered her face with her hands. "I have a confession to make."

She felt Mia and Artemis lean in. "Yeah?" they asked in unison.

"I've been dreaming all this time." She squeezed her eyes shut. "About . . . Joe Hatcher."

"Aha! I knew it!" Mia squealed.

Was it that obvious? Caroline parted her fingers and looked out with one eye. "You knew what?"

"That you were dreaming." Mia pointed an accusing

finger. "Okay, now spill. Exactly what is Joe doing to you? How kinky was it? I want details."

"Well, I have to say that I'm not surprised," Artemis cut in. "The way you act around him is—"

"How do I act?" Dread kicked her right in the stomach. She searched her friends' expressions, hoping she didn't find what she suspected. "Please tell me that I'm not acting like—"

"A goofball." Mia finished bluntly.

Artemis scrunched her nose at the term. "No, more like a dork."

"Oh, no!" The dread ate away at her until she wanted to gag on it. "That can't be happening," she said in a horrified whisper.

"What's wrong with that?" Mia looked at Artemis for clarification, but the other woman frowned with confusion. "I'm sure Joe finds it cute."

"Argh!" She shoved the heels of her hands into her eyes. "This is bad. This is really bad." She dropped her hands and gave a pleading look to her friends. "What am I going to do? I have to get some sleep, but every time I close my eyes, I see Joe. Hard and naked." She swallowed roughly as she remembered.

"Yeah?" Mia perked up. "How long is he?"

"Excuse me,"—Artemis held her hand up like a traffic cop—"but what is wrong with having sex with Joe?"

"Because when I'm around him, I get goofy." Weren't they paying any attention?

Artemis's eyes drifted up as she processed the reason, but apparently it didn't compute with her. "And that's . . . bad?"

"Yeah!"

"I don't understand," Artemis said.

"Me, either," Mia admitted.

Caroline was reluctant to tell her friends more, but she wanted them to understand. Needed them to. She leaned back in the cafeteria booth and folded her arms across her chest. "I was a nerd until college."

Mia's mouth fell open. "Shut up!"

Caroline looked away and focused on the bizarre design of the linoleum floor. "It's true. I suffered. A lot." She tightened her arms around her. "I'm happy with the way I am now. I'm never going to be a nerd again. But when I'm around Joe, I revert back."

"You were a nerd?" Mia's voice raised a notch.

"Shh!" Caroline quickly looked around the cafeteria before dropping her voice. "I'm serious. I don't want to advertise it."

"Yeah, Mia." Artemis frowned and gave a little shake to her head. "It was obviously a painful experience for Caroline. No need to bring it up again."

"Okay, fine." Mia slouched back in her chair and pursed her lips for about a second. "Do you have an old school picture?"

"No," Caroline lied. "I tore them all up and burned the scraps." All of them except for one. The worst of the lot. It was so bad that it could still bring her to tears.

She probably should have burned it with the rest, but something had held her back. As much as she wanted to erase the past, she knew that forgetting would be fatal. She kept the picture hidden deep in her jewelry box and brought it out when she needed a harsh reminder.

"I think I know of a way to stop dreaming about Joe," Artemis said.

"You do?" Caroline latched onto that. Things were suddenly looking up. "Are you going to put a spell on me?"

Artemis's jaw slid to one side as she reined in her patience. "For the last time, I am not doing any spells for either of you."

"But this is an emergency." Caroline knew she was close to whining, but she wasn't above it at this moment.

Patting Caroline's arm with a comforting hand, Artemis said, "The quickest way to stop dreaming about Joe is to sleep with him."

Caroline wasn't sure if she heard right. "This is your plan?" She suspected that Artemis had been hanging around Mia too much lately.

"Yeah!" Mia pumped her fist. "All right! Now we're talking!"

"No, no." She had to stop them before she devised her seduction strategy. "I don't agree with this plan."

"Think about it, Caroline," Artemis said. "You've avoided thinking about Joe. Instead of pushing him out of your mind, you've made him even more attractive. He's your forbidden fruit."

"She has a point," Mia said.

"I disagree." Caroline shook her head. "I like my idea of avoiding him at all costs, thereby forgetting what he looks like."

"And how are you going to do that?" Artemis asked. "That is not going to happen with the two of you working together. And it's not like you're going to quit your job over him."

It was true. She would never quit her job over a man, even one as dangerous to her way of life as Joe Hatcher. "So what you're saying is that in order to get a good night's sleep, I have to . . ."

Artemis's lips twitched with a suppressed smile. "Sleep with Joe."

"Sounds like a plan to me." Mia rubbed her hands together. "When are you going to jump him?"

"I'm not." Caroline had made up her mind. "It's too risky. I'll come up with a plan that doesn't involve sex."

Joe turned the corner to the conference room just as Caroline Mitchell appeared from the other direction. Desire gripped him until he was rendered motionless. He watched her silently, heat invading and saturating his veins.

Crackling with energy, Caroline hurried down the hallway with eye-catching confidence. Her long, black hair streamed behind her as she walked. The ivory blouse and dark, slim skirt should have made her look prim, but nothing could dampen Caroline's vitality.

His gaze collided with hers and she stumbled to a halt. He wondered if she was going to ignore him, make a run for it or acknowledge his existence. He decided to make it easier for her.

"Caroline," he greeted and held the door for her.

"Joe," she finally said and hurried across the threshold. "I didn't know you were going to be in this meeting."

"Since we're creating the same product line together," Joe said as he followed her into the conference room, "I think it's a safe bet we will be seeing a lot of each other for the next few months." He pulled the chair out for her. "Take a seat."

Her hesitation hung in the air, but she swiftly accepted the inevitable. "Thank you."

As Joe slid her chair closer to the table, he leaned down and inhaled her scent. It kicked him in the gut and clawed at his hunger for her. "So what are you doing Friday night?" he said softly in her ear.

Her shoulders sagged wearily. "I know I'm not going out with you."

"True, because I would have worn you out by then," he replied as he took the chair next to hers. "You'll need to catch up on your rest sometime."

A smile played on her lips and slowly grew. Joe found himself smiling along with her. Why did that simple sight give him so much pleasure? Why did her smile make him feel young and powerful?

"You just never give up, do you?" Caroline looked at him from beneath her long lashes.

The eye move was flirty and feminine. Joe held back his instinctive male response, knowing it wasn't the right time to unleash the intensity he felt. "Not when I want something, or someone, bad enough," he said gruffly.

"And when you *don't* get what you want, what do you do?" Caroline asked. She seemed interested in his answer as she rested her elbow against the back of her chair.

"I always get what I want." And while what he said was true, he wondered if Caroline was going to break his perfect record.

"Let's say you get a night with me." Caroline frowned, probably realizing how suggestive, how probable it sounded. "Hypothetically speaking."

Joe rolled his eyes. "Of course."

"How would you spend it?"

A thousand images crowded his mind and his muscles clenched. He bit his bottom lip to prevent from leering, but he knew it was too late. If Caroline's smirk was anything to go by, she knew the power she had over him.

"I would spend every moment fulfilling your fantasies," he said, wrestling for control over his body's responses.

"Oh, good answer," she mocked, and softly clapped her hands. "But what about your fantasies? After all, you only get one night."

"The night is my fantasy," he said in all seriousness. "What occurs during that night is about your fantasies."

Her lips parted in surprise. "You don't even know what my fantasies are."

"Doesn't matter."

He saw something wicked flash in her eyes.

"For all you know, I could be into some painful stuff."

"If I have to take you over my knee, so be it." He clasped his hand over his chest. "I'll make the sacrifice."

Caroline leaned closer. "I meant I would administer the pain to you." She took one look at his dumbfounded expression and laughed out loud.

The other executives in the room jerked with surprise as they heard Caroline's belly laugh. Fortunately, they hadn't heard the rest. Joe had to admit her laugh wasn't at all what he'd expected. It was loud and rusty and she put her whole body in it.

Joe's wide smile froze. He felt kicked off the edge of safety and about to fall in love. It was a scary, thrilling ride. He just hoped it didn't end with him splattered on the ground, and walked on. First he had to get to the first night and live through it.

"Okay," he said, "we obviously need a few guidelines."

"Aw." Caroline gave an exaggerated pout. "What's the fun in that?"

"We can rule out anything that might cause me long-term emotional and physical damage. I'm sure you have enough fantasies that will last us the entire night. Legal and consensual fantasies." Hmm . . . those broad guidelines could still get him into trouble. "For the record, I'm not consenting to cross-dressing."

Caroline snorted with laughter. Her eyes bulged at the sound. She clapped her hand over her face and muffled her nose and mouth.

"Come to think of it,"—Joe tapped his chin playfully—"that still leaves us with potentially hundreds of fantasies but maybe twelve hours. At most. I won't complain if our night spills into another night. Or even another night."

Caroline cleared her throat and regained her composure. "And I repeat, this is hypothetically speaking," she said in a cool tone.

Whoa. Joe blinked and stared at her. One minute she was flirting with him and then the frost hit. What caused that attitude change?

He considered the possibilities when it dawned on him. He got too greedy. That was the problem. When was he ever going to learn? She wanted only one night and he was already planning their future together.

He had to repair the damage somehow, Joe decided as the company's president entered the room and started the meeting. Because he wasn't going to let this setback hurt his goal. He didn't care how greedy he was—Caroline Mitchell would be his by the end of the month.

Sheesh! Well, there went her plan to avoid Joe Hatcher. And her don't-mess-with-me image had just gone out the window. What was she thinking, flirting with him and discussing sexual fantasies?

She hadn't been thinking. She was going with what felt good. What felt right.

And then she'd laughed in front of him. She never let loose with her laugh. Never. Of course, she'd had to top it all off by snorting. Snorting! Caroline felt the blush crawling up her neck and flooding her cheeks. She'd given that up years ago along with her programmable digital wristwatch.

But the idea of Joe in a dress was priceless. He was far too masculine and too arrogant. Even now, as the president droned on in front of her about focus groups, Caroline had to stifle a chuckle.

Hey! Maybe that was the way to get over Joe. Imagining him in a dress was riskier than mentally reciting the periodic table, but more effective. And it would be like those who suffer stage fright who have to imagine their audience naked.

Her stomach flipped. Naked . . . with him . . . for him . . .

Why did she have to think about getting naked with Joe? Especially with him sitting right next to her?! Caroline screwed her eyes shut, warding off the image, but it was too strong and she was too needy.

She easily imagined Joe getting up from his seat and standing behind her chair. The company president droned on and the fantasy really got going. . .

She tried to see what he was doing, but his hands settled

at the base of her neck. The fine hairs on her nape prickled as he kept her facing straight ahead with the dominating touch of his fingers.

His hands drifted to her shoulders, kneading the tension from her muscles. Caroline would have melted under his touch, but her gaze darted around the room. No one noticed what was going on.

His hand trailed down her shoulders before dipping inside her blouse. She gasped in surprise as Joe's fingers sought her breast. He pressed his mouth against the frantic pulse in her throat. Caroline arched, wanting more.

He freed her breast from its lacy confines. Caroline swallowed a groan as Joe's rough hand scratched her soft skin. She had to cry out when he grasped her nipple between his fingers and pinched hard. The white-hot sensations forked through her body like lightning.

Startled, Caroline bolted from her seat. Her sudden move didn't interrupt the meeting around her. She felt invisible but on the verge of being exposed.

But she didn't want people to know how much she craved Joe's hands on her. All over her, exploring every crevice and hollow. Finding and giving pleasure, without anything barring his journey.

She whirled around and faced him. Whatever she was going to say lodged in her throat when she saw his expression. No longer the cosmopolitan businessman or the sophisticated lover, Joe Hatcher's eyes glittered with an elemental message that made her womb ripple in response.

He grabbed the back of her head and kissed her hard. Her heart thudded as she opened her mouth to his primitive claim. She was desperate for him to claim her body and soul, but at the same time it frightened her.

The edge of the conference table bit into her thighs. She grabbed his necktie, but it served poorly as a leash as Joe's ruthless fingers tore at her blouse.

Cool air wafted over her skin. Caroline yanked her mouth

away and looked over her shoulder to find her blouse strewn on the polished tabletop. Her bra sailed in the air and landed near the pool of silk.

She was suddenly lying on the conference table, her hair fanned around her head. Joe stripped her naked, leaving her momentarily stunned and confused. Caroline looked around with wild eyes.

The meeting continued. Huang's voice droned on about numbers until they jumbled in her mind. Her coworkers spoke around, over and through her nude body, which was displayed spread-eagled on the giant table.

At the sound of metal scraping, Caroline jerked her head back to Joe. He unzipped his trousers, but remained fully clothed. The sight of her nudity against his expensive suit made her feel wanton and wicked.

Hooking her legs under his hands, Joe drew her bottom to the edge of the table. With one swift move, he entered her wet core. Caroline's hips lurched from the table as he filled and stretched her. Lust scorched her skin, growing hotter as he began to thrust. As he began to thrust, her nails scored the polished table.

Joe's face grew harsh and feral with each powerful stroke. A keening cry escaped from her as her fingernails scored the polished table. The climax wound tight and sleek in her body, ready to spiral out of control.

"Caroline."

She felt everyone turn. Knew they saw her naked and writhing under Joe. The heat of their eyes sputtered across her skin and fed her desire.

The climax lit her body. She crashed through a kaleidoscope of colors and faces. Flying through a tunnel at warp speed, she fell back in her seat with a jolt.

And all eyes around the conference table were on her. She quickly glanced down. Whew. Her blouse and skirt were still on, but she was achy and tight as small tremors wracked her body.

Joe gave her a kick from under the table.

She jumped and faced the company president. "Yes?"

"Good." Huang nodded briskly. "We will expect your e-mail updating us by the end of the day. That's all for today, people."

E-mail? What e-mail? She looked around, disoriented. Her coworkers got up from their seats and from the low, industrious murmur of their voices, it didn't sound like anything was amiss.

Which could only mean one thing. Caroline's chest tightened with dread as she grudgingly faced the facts. Her dreams were now invading her waking moments.

She was having erotic daydreams. It was unbelievable, but true. At work, no less. During important meetings.

Caroline sighed with defeat. She had to do something about it. Something now before she lost her job over daydreaming.

And that something had to be Joe.

"What are you doing tonight?"

Joe stiffened and glanced at Caroline. Had he heard right? Was she asking him out? That wasn't possible.

He looked behind him, just in case she was talking to some other guy. No one else was left in the conference room, which was good. He didn't relish the idea of getting jealous and maiming certain body parts of his coworkers.

Glancing back at Caroline, his gaze collided with her cool one. "Are you asking for a date tonight?" he asked, pleased that his voice didn't crack.

"No." Caroline was emphatic.

"No, of course not," he said wryly, scooping up his papers. What had he been thinking?

"I'm asking you to bed," she corrected him.

"Bed?" The papers crinkled under his fingers.

"Let's make it my bed." She turned to leave.

Wow. He wasn't imagining things. She really had said bed. Twice. "Okay."

"No," she swung back, "let's make it yours."

"Tonight?" Not that he would quibble over the details, but he wanted to lock her in before she changed her mind.

A small frown puckered between her eyebrows. "Do you already have plans?"

If he did, they were as good as canceled. "No."

"Good. Then I'll meet you at your place after dinner. Seven o'clock sharp," she decided briskly and strode toward the door.

"O . . . kay." After dinner. Not a date. She didn't need to beat him over the head with her point. Could she be any more blunt about the invitation? He knew she wanted it all to be about sex and nothing else. She didn't want anything to do with him other than what occurred in his bed.

He also knew that he didn't want that kind of offer. He wanted everything. But was it better to take what he could get and hope for more? Joe had a feeling she would not make another offer if he rejected this one. "Wait a second."

She paused and slowly looked over her shoulder. "Yes?" Caroline didn't look so certain anymore.

"What changed your mind?"

Caroline waved off the question with the flick of her hand. "You're getting your fantasy. Does it really matter?"

"Yes." Because his fantasy meant that she wanted him just as much as he wanted her. That wasn't the case at all. He felt like she'd just crossed his name off her to-do list.

"I have more fantasies than I realized. Why wait around when I can make it happen right now?" she asked as she exited the conference room.

"Why, indeed?" he muttered to himself, staring at the

empty doorway. The message was clear. He wasn't the fantasy, but the tool to achieve her fantasy. Ouch.

Fine. Joe's eyes narrowed. He would make his fantasy happen, too. By tomorrow morning, she'd want him more than ever.

Chapter 3

I have lost my mind, Caroline decided as she paced around her office. *That has to be it. I've completely lost it.* After all, what made her think she could experience a night of sex with Joe Hatcher and leave emotionally unscathed with him none the wiser?

Lust. Pure and simple lust. Because she really, really wanted Joe, for one moment—of course, it had to be the *wrong* moment—she allowed herself to believe she could handle him.

But she couldn't handle the idea of him seeing certain aspects of her personality. The humiliating aspects. The unlovable ones. Basically, the nerdy aspects.

The possibility was actually a high probability. It wasn't like she had always been geekiness-free during sex. There were a few unguarded moments that could have been classified as . . . nerdish.

But that was different. The guys didn't notice. They were too busy making their own fantasies come true. This time, Joe was going to focus all of his attention on her.

He was bound to notice. Maybe he wouldn't care . . .

Yeah, right. Caroline made a face at her own naïveté. Joe was expecting a bombshell in his bed, not a brainiac.

She had to stop freaking out and do something about it.

But what? What could she possibly do before seven o'clock that night? She would need a miracle. Or magic.

Magic. Caroline stiffened and lunged for the phone.

Quickly punching in Artemis's office number, she sighed with relief when her friend answered. "Artemis, I need your help."

"You got it."

"I need a magic potion recipe." The words rushed out of her. She couldn't believe she, a woman who believed in science, was asking for magical assistance. She couldn't believe that it made absolute sense. It was yet another sign that she had lost her mind.

"Caroline Mitchell!" Artemis nearly yelled. "As I have told Mia a gazillion times, witches are strictly forbidden to create love potions."

"I—"

"And do you know why?" Artemis asked. "I'll tell you why. Because they can cause harm."

"I know that—"

"And any action you do to a person has a tendency to turn around and bite you in the butt. And with more teeth than whatever you did first."

Caroline knew she had to interrupt before she received a full lecture. "Do you have a recipe that I can use that will emphasize some parts of me and conceal other parts?"

"Now that I can do." Artemis immediately swerved onto a different mental track. "What are you looking for? You want something to make your boobs bigger?"

"No." She glanced down at her chest. "What's wrong with them?"

"Nothing! That's usually what women want to emphasize. What are you trying to make bigger?"

"Not exactly bigger." Caroline hedged. She knew she had to tell Artemis all of her plans. "I have a, uh, date tonight with Joe."

Artemis squealed. She reached a decibel that threatened to shatter Caroline's ear. "Stop it, Artemis. Stop . . . I mean it."

"Why do you need a potion?" Artemis asked, excitement blurring her voice. "Joe is ready to jump in your bed."

"Yeah, but he'll notice *everything*."

"Everything? Oh!" she exclaimed. "You mean your inner geek."

Caroline winced. "I need something to hide that one part of me. Do you have anything? Anything I can make before tonight?"

"As a matter of fact, I just might. I'll have to go look it up. But if I remember right, it requires a few unusual ingredients."

"Not a problem." Caroline knew she could jump that hurdle easily. "I have an entire aromatherapy lab at my disposal."

"Great. I'll e-mail you the recipe and incantation as soon as I find it," Artemis promised.

"Incantation?" Her friend could not be serious.

"It's a chant. And before you even ask, you can't skip that part. Otherwise the potion won't work."

It was too much of a risk to skip that step. She would have to do the chant. She wouldn't like it, but she'd do it. "You mean I have to act like a geek to stop being one?" Caroline teased.

"Funny. Do you want the recipe?" A threatening tone crept into Artemis's voice.

"Yes, please," she said meekly. It probably wasn't wise to tease someone who had the power to turn her into a frog. Caroline wasn't going to test her friend's belief in the biting-butt karma.

"And I expect details at the Dream Circle tomorrow," Artemis informed her.

"What are you talking about?" Caroline asked as she automatically glanced at her calendar. "We just had one today."

"I'm calling an emergency Dream Circle so we can find out if reality matched fantasy."

Caroline's stomach twisted. "Oh, great. Thanks a lot. I'm so glad to know I'm walking into this night with absolutely no pressure."

Joe shoved the sleeves of his jersey to his elbows and surveyed his condo. He didn't want it to look like a bachelor's lair, but he wanted to bring a seductive atmosphere to the night. After so many changes and so much second-guessing, he wasn't sure if he had accomplished his goal.

He couldn't believe he was finally going to make love to Caroline Mitchell. After all this time of waiting, it was almost happening too fast. It was almost too good to be true.

No. Joe felt his chest expand as he took a steady breath. He wasn't going to psych himself out of this. He was going to make this a night to remember. Make it so good that Caroline would want her fantasies to last forever.

Joe set the lights low just as the doorbell rang. Fiery excitement slammed through him and he almost controlled the shudder that rippled through him. He had to play it smooth or he'd mess up. He knew without a doubt that Caroline would never give him another chance.

Swinging the door open, he saw Caroline standing on the other side. He was glad he was hanging onto the doorknob. Otherwise he would have fallen onto his knees and begged for mercy.

Caroline wore a short black raincoat tied snugly around her waist. The dark color emphasized the paleness of her skin. A lot of skin. A lot of bare skin. He couldn't tell if she wore anything under the coat and his mind buzzed at the possibility.

"Hi." His voice sounded hoarse.

"Hi," she repeated. Her hand fluttered to her face and

she pressed her finger along the bridge of her nose. She quickly brushed back the hair from her forehead.

"Come on in." He stepped back, his gaze roving over her sleek body as she stepped inside. His attention dropped to her shoes as they clicked against the hardwood floor. The aggressively pointed toe and impossibly thin heels made them look lethal. Much like their owner.

Joe glanced up as Caroline untied her belt. His cock grew hard and heavy as the straps fell to her sides. His mouth grew painfully dry as she peeled the black raincoat away from her curves.

He blinked when she uncovered a short, skin-tight red dress. The fabric lovingly hugged every inch from her shoulders to the top of her thighs. Joe leaned heavily against the door for support. "You're beautiful."

She dipped her square chin almost shyly. "Thank you."

He took the coat from her hands. "Would you like something to drink?" He knew he could use something that would clear his head.

"No, I would like something like this," she said, and stepped up to him. The aggression and fire in her eyes matched how he felt. She flattened her palms on the door by his head and kissed him.

Fireworks exploded inside him. When she darted her tongue inside his mouth, hot sparks shot through his blood, falling, tripping and catching his body on fire before pooling in his groin.

Caroline leaned into him. Her breasts nestled into his chest as her hips bumped against his. Her softness nearly undid him.

He noticed something different about her scent. It was spicy. Exotic, like her heat that surrounded him.

Her coat dropped from his hands and he wrapped his arms around her. He needed her closer, needed to be part of her. He explored the curve of her back and the jut of her hips, feeling the tremors under his fingertips.

He wanted to bury himself in her. Right here, right now, right against the door. But that would end the fantasy before it even started. If he wanted to give her a night to remember, it was going to require some finesse. Something he wasn't feeling right now.

Caroline moaned and shimmied against him. Joe's knees weakened. Maybe he should hurry things along before he did something stupid—like collapse in a heap.

She seemed to have the same idea. "Take me to bed," she ordered against his lips. "Now."

Okay, there went his whole seduction scene. Even though he knew why she was there, he had wanted to make it special—wine, candlelight, soft dance music.

Caroline retreated and opened her eyes. He wasn't sure what he saw. Her knowing smirk could mean anything. He decided it was a good thing.

"Fine, I'll take you to bed."

She hooked her finger in his shirt and led him away from the door.

Her brazen attitude made him hot—hotter than he could remember. There was something incredibly sexy about a woman who knew what she wanted and wasn't afraid to go for it. Especially when he was her goal. Joe was more than ready to strip and let her have her way with him.

"Nice view," she commented, tilting her head at the wall of windows in his living room. The lights of the Seattle skyline twinkled through the rainy night.

Joe didn't comment. He was too preoccupied by the sway of her hips. He swiped his tongue across his lips in anticipation.

Caroline glanced over her shoulder, almost as if she was checking to see if she still had his attention. Like that was going to be a problem. "Did you know that the Space Needle is six hundred and five feet high?" she said in a sudden rush.

"Uh, no." He didn't want her to think of gigantic proportions just now. At least not in terms of feet, when she was going to be dealing with inches very soon.

"And it was built in 1962 as part of the World's Fair . . ." Her eyes widened and she immediately stopped talking. She did that cute thing with her tongue between her teeth.

Maybe she was nervous. Good. He wanted to let out a gigantic sigh of relief. If she was nervous, then this night meant something to her. He clung to that hope.

The magic potion seemed to be working. Joe didn't notice her slipups. Caroline gave another sly look at him as her heart pumped nervously. He seemed positively mesmerized.

Now if only the potion could guide her into making this night a success. While it disguised her nerdiness, she still felt like one. A big, fat geeky one.

Caroline's bold stride into his condo shuffled to a stop. Studying all the doors in the hallway, she had no idea where his bedroom was. *Way to go. What's your encore going to be? Get lost in his closet?*

She turned and her heel caught the rug's fringe border. Pitching forward, Caroline grabbed hold of Joe. His hands clasped her elbows before she could gasp.

But she wasn't finished falling, apparently. The sound of ripping fabric filled the air. Caroline closed her eyes and prayed. *Please don't let that be anything of mine.*

She opened her eyes and saw fragments of Joe's shirt in her hands. Horror filled her but she determinedly kept her expression clear. She glanced up and her gaze slammed into his. His green eyes glittered with lust. And amusement.

Cover me, she silently begged the magic potion. She had a feeling this fell out of the magic's jurisdiction. It was time to use some bravado.

"I've been wanting to tear your clothes off." She threw the scraps on the floor. Somehow that didn't sound convincing.

Joe stepped forward and she felt her nerves fluttering like butterflies on speed. "Wait." She stepped back and kicked off her heels. Caroline quickly removed her dress and revealed that she wore nothing underneath.

She stood before him naked. Her skin prickled as her nipples tightened under his intense gaze. She felt the dampness grow between her legs. Her strategy had been that if he saw her body, he would be blind to her actions.

In theory, that might have worked. In reality, she still felt like a nerd. A naked nerd, at that. "Now you can take me to bed."

She placed her hands on her hips when she really wanted to cover herself with them. "Don't you want to take me to bed?" she asked him with just a tad of aggression.

"I want to make love to you," Joe corrected her. His calm certainty made her more nervous.

"Semantics, schmantics," she muttered. Strange—in all of her dreams, Joe never talked. "Isn't this night about my fantasies?"

He shrugged his shoulders. "Tell me one."

The light played on the defined muscles. She felt the quivering low in her belly. Maybe she was reacting to his self-confidence. It made her feel like he was in charge, and she couldn't let that happen. She needed to throw him a challenge. Something real good. Something that would shut him up quickly.

She felt sly as an idea popped in her head. "There are sixty-four positions in the *Kama Sutra*," she informed him. "I want you to do all of them with me."

"Tonight?" His voice cracked.

"Yeah, all of them tonight. We better start now."

Joe walked toward her. Her uncertainty bloomed wider with each step. When his feet touched hers, she reluctantly trailed her gaze from his amazing chest to his green eyes.

He leaned down and for one breathless moment she thought he was going to kiss her. She parted her lips in anticipation. His mouth grazed her as she felt his hands on her waist.

Without warning, he lifted her up. Caroline squawked in surprise as he hooked her legs around his waist. She grabbed for his shoulders as his hands held her back.

"What are you doing?" His belt scratched the soft flesh of her thighs.

"Taking you to bed," he replied as he strode to the end of the hall. "Isn't that what you want?"

"Just checking. This is the exact position of the Congress of the Vine. I didn't know if you were planning to do that first."

His gaze didn't leave her face as he carried her to the bedroom. Caroline felt like he saw everything. Like he could see inside her and knew what made her tick. She was so thankful for the potion or she would have been already in a freaking-out mode.

Joe stopped at the edge of the bed. Caroline frowned as he slowly lowered her onto the firm mattress. She had been expecting something rough and playful, not soft and gentle.

She was about to pull him down on top of her when his hands went to his belt. Caroline's mouth went dry as he stripped off his trousers and boxers. Her eyes widened at the sight of his cock. He was already fully aroused and his length stood proudly before her.

Caroline reached out to touch him, but Joe stopped her. "No," he said in a husky voice. "Not yet. But I can touch you."

He caressed her everywhere. Her skin burned for him.

It was too sensitive to withstand his tender touch, yet too painful to withdraw. A fine sheen of sweat covered her body by the time Joe dipped his fingers into her slit.

"Joe!" She bucked and swayed. "Take me now."

He reached for the bedside table and grabbed a condom. After he slid it on, Joe knelt between her legs. He placed his forearms on the mattress below her shoulders.

"Open your legs wide, but hold onto my waist and thighs," he coached Caroline. "Don't rest on the bed. I'll support you."

She arched her spine and hips. Only her head and shoulders lay on the bed. But he still didn't enter her.

"Joe," she whimpered as an unbearable tension rested low in her belly. "Please."

"Kiss me first," he ordered.

"Joe." She was past the point of foreplay. She wanted him in her. Now.

He wouldn't be persuaded. "Kiss me."

She blindly sought his mouth. As her lips touched his, she moaned at the raw electricity arcing between them. She cupped his face with her hands and drove her tongue into his mouth. The wet, messy, wild kisses made her greedy. Voracious.

Joe slid his cock into her wetness, claiming her at a deep angle. His pelvis rubbed against her clit, driving her to the brink of insanity. She was open, vulnerable and dependent on him for her pleasure. It wasn't her fantasy, but her dreams paled in comparison to how he made her feel.

He kept up the relentless rhythm for what seemed like forever. Caroline's muscles shook and burned. She was desperate for the agonizing spiral of sensations to end. To keep going. To take her to another level.

"Joe. I'm going to . . ." She felt like she was falling. Imploding. Her soul dissolved with joy as Joe gave one final thrust before gathering her in his arms.

Caroline lay in his embrace. Stunned. Destroyed. Joe

lifted his head and looked into her eyes. She couldn't look away. She felt the flash of a connection and it held. The moment scared her. Comforted her.

Joe paused. She could tell he was about to say something. Caroline braced herself, hoping it wasn't something too intimate.

"Sixty-three more to go," he announced. His smile was smug and brash.

Oh, God. Her replying smile was weak in comparison. *Me and my big mouth. What did I get myself into?*

His alarm blared to life. Joe reached over and slapped the clock into silence. Groaning as he turned onto his back, Joe couldn't remember a time when he'd felt so exhausted. Every inch of his body ached. It was a good ache, but an ache just the same.

It was a struggle to turn his head and open his eyes, but the sight was worth it: Caroline sprawled on his bed, naked and exhausted. She took over the bed, the sheets tangled around her, her tousled hair shrouding her face.

He gently brushed her silky hair away from her cheek and tucked it behind her ear. His heart squeezed as he revealed her face. He wanted to wake up every morning to her, but that wasn't the deal.

That didn't mean he was going to let the deal stand. No way. He had to come up with a campaign to get another night with her. And then another . . .

Wrapping an arm around her small waist, he curled her against him. She instinctively nuzzled against his chest. "Joe." Caroline's contented murmur warmed him with hope.

"Yeah?" His mouth was against her ear.

She suddenly stiffened. "Joe!" She looked up abruptly, almost hitting his jaw with her head. "Uh . . . what time is it?" she asked as she grabbed for the sheets.

"Six in the morning," he murmured as he covered her mouth with small, soft kisses.

"It's worn off," she said almost to herself.

"Hmm?" His tongue outlined the curve of her bottom lip.

Caroline dodged away. "Um, my, m-makeup has worn off." Her hands fluttered in front of her face. "I probably have raccoon eyes."

"You look beautiful." He swooped down for another kiss.

Caroline rolled away. Not realizing she was so close to the edge of the bed, she lost her balance. She yelped as her arms and legs flailed. Joe was a second too late to grab her. She hit the floor with a thud.

"Ouch," she said dully.

Joe grimaced, knowing that had to hurt more than she let on. "Are you okay?" He peered over the edge of the bed. She was face up, but didn't look at him.

"I need to leave," she said, her face blank of expression as she stared up at the ceiling.

"No, you don't." He reached for her.

"I have to go back to my place and get ready for work." Caroline awkwardly stood up but the bedsheet refused to cooperate with her plans.

"Let's call in sick."

"No, I can't." She scooped the sheet off the floor.

"Come on, Caroline." The hope he'd felt earlier was shriveling up.

She held the sheet in front of her like a shield. "Our agreement was for one night and one night only," she reminded him briskly as she headed for the bathroom.

"So that's it?" he called out to her.

She hesitated, and Joe's dying hope swelled to life.

"Yeah," she said. "That's it." She closed the door behind her.

Great. Joe flopped back on the bed. He had made the most of his chance but it wasn't good enough. She didn't want a repeat performance. She didn't want one more night.

He glared outside the window. The gray morning and steady rain hitting the windowpanes matched his mood. At least the sun didn't make a rare appearance and cheerfully mock him.

Joe tensed as an idea hit him sideways. Caroline didn't want one more night, but there was no agreement made about one afternoon. Or one morning . . . one weekend for that matter.

Chapter 4

"Details, Caroline," Mia said that afternoon after they found a booth in the corner of the cafeteria. She opened her soda can and took a big gulp. "Every last one of them, and don't leave anything out."

"Forget the details," Caroline said, snapping her paper napkin open before placing it on her lap. "I've got a major crisis going on."

Mia gasped. "Did the condom break?"

"Worse." She groaned and covered her eyes with her hands. "It was absolutely the most amazing night of my life."

"Uh-huh," Mia said, her eyes squinting with incomprehension. "What's wrong with that?"

Caroline closed her eyes like a kid wishing on a star. "I really, really, really want another night with Joe."

"And he doesn't want it?" Mia commiserated.

"No, he wants it." Caroline dropped her hands and made an attempt to eat. "He suggested we call in sick today, but I said no."

"No? You said no." Mia shook her head in dismay. "Did you fall on your head last night?"

She didn't want to think about how she fell off the bed.

Just her luck it happened once the potion had worn off. "Almost."

"Really?" Mia's eyebrows shot up.

"Caroline," Artemis interrupted before the conversation disintegrated into another how-to sex talk, "I don't understand what the problem is."

"I'm falling for him," she confessed in a whisper. "Big time."

"Oh," Mia said, a wealth of understanding suffusing the word. She reached over the table and patted Caroline's hand in an attempt to offer some comfort.

"But I can't risk it," Caroline said with some regret. She pushed the lettuce leaves around her plate with her fork. "I can't handle the rejection when he finds out all about me. And rejection is inevitable."

"True," Mia said with her usual bluntness. "He is sophistication personified."

"Hey, you guys aren't even giving him a chance," Artemis said to them accusingly. "Have you ever considered that he might love everything about you?"

"There are a lot of things about me that just aren't lovable." And Caroline knew firsthand that no one could love a nerd. They definitely couldn't desire one.

"Bull," Mia said. "I like you, even on your bad days. So does Artemis."

"That's different and you know it," Caroline said.

Her friends didn't argue and they fell into a silence. Caroline stared at her salad, unable to eat. All she could do was remember her night with Joe.

"So how good is he?" Mia broke the silence.

"Mia!" Caroline and Artemis said in unison.

"What?" She hunched her shoulders in defense. "I want to know."

"Please, you guys," Artemis pleaded, dropping her fork onto her plate. "I don't want to know if he uses a Morse code rhythm or if he has any tattoos."

"You know all that info about everyone else," Mia pointed out self-righteously.

Artemis motioned to herself. "I work for Joe. I'd rather not know."

"Okay, okay. Fine. I won't ask for specifics," Mia said as she took another sip of soda. "But what does he sound like when he comes?"

"Mia!" Artemis said, fully exasperated.

"Generally speaking," Mia clarified as she set her soda can down. "Not specifically."

"I really don't want to . . ." Caroline leaned back and rested her head against the booth and sighed with defeat. "I can't talk about it."

"That good, huh?" Mia said. Her lips twisted as she considered the facts. "So he's back on the market, right?"

Jealousy stabbed her in the chest. The fury left her raw and bleeding. "No, he is *not* available," she replied coldly through clenched teeth.

"Meow."

"Come on, Mia. You know the unwritten rule. You don't sleep with a friend's present or former boyfriend, lover, fiancé or husband."

Mia turned and faced Artemis. "Do you realize that rule means you are ineligible to date any single male at this company?"

Artemis rolled her eyes. "What I do in the name of friendship," she replied dryly.

"And that rule does not apply to one-night stands," Mia added.

Artemis disagreed. "A one-night stand is a lover. The point of that one night is sex. What does a lover do? Have sex."

"No, no, no." Mia shook her head vigorously. "A lover means a relationship. A one-night stand is the opposite of a relationship."

"Well, for all we know, Caroline might want a relationship with Joe," Artemis argued back.

Mia and Artemis turned to Caroline. They quietly waited for her answer. She looked away from their questioning looks.

"Well, that's the sixty-thousand dollar question, isn't it? I don't know." Caroline felt the pressure to make the difficult decision. "I seduced Joe to purge him from my mind, but it didn't work out that way. Now I want more of him!"

Joe sat on the other side of the booth. His hands clenched the edges of his newspaper, the print blurring in front of his eyes. He felt a burning sensation deep in his gut.

He wasn't surprised to hear how adamant Caroline was about last night being a one-night stand. She'd made it perfectly clear this morning. But her reasons cut him to the quick.

I seduced Joe to purge him from my mind. . . .

He hoped she failed her objective. Spectacularly. He wanted their night together to occupy her dreams for the rest of her life.

Problem was, it would haunt him, too.

"What prompted you to seduce him in the first place?" he heard Artemis ask. "You were determined to stay clear of any sex with Joe."

"Yeah, until I started having daydreams about him at the most inopportune moments!" Caroline said. "One minute I'm sitting next to him at the conference room, and the next minute I have this daydream of him taking me right on the table with everyone watching me."

The conference table? Joe immediately pictured himself lying on the table as Caroline hiked up her business suit and straddled him. She would be hot and wet as she sheathed his cock. She would ride him with abandon, screaming her release. . . .

"Interesting," Artemis commented thoughtfully. "Do you often have dreams about exhibitionism?"

"Now is not the time for dream interpretation," Caroline said. "I need some advice. What should I do about this need I have about Joe? Should I go cold turkey? Maybe cut out my zinc intake to lower my sex drive? What do you think?"

"It's obvious." Even with a booth between them, Joe could easily hear Artemis's bossiness. "You are nipping the attraction in the bud too early. You need to let it take its natural course."

"You mean . . . ?"

"You have to bed him again," he heard Mia say. "Often. Frequently. Round the clock. As long as it takes to get him out of your system."

Joe hissed at the thought of having sex around the clock with Caroline. The newspaper rattled in his hands. His cock hardened as sweat broke out on his forehead. He didn't know how much more of the conversation he could take.

"I don't like that answer," Caroline replied. "Artemis, what do you think I should do?"

"As impossible as it may seem, I agree with Mia. Take Joe to your bed and don't let him out until you've had your fill."

"I . . . I don't know," Caroline said. "I'll have to think about it."

Joe didn't have to think about it at all, he decided as he folded the newspaper with a crisp snap. He would not be making love to Caroline. If she thought it was going to be easy to crawl back into his bed, she was in for a big surprise.

It didn't matter how much he wanted Caroline. How much he loved her and wanted her to love him.

I seduced Joe to purge him from my mind . . .

He winced and decided he'd make it real simple for her. After all, she managed to destroy the one fantasy he had. The one that had her wanting him as much as he wanted her. That's what he got for finally dreaming of something that could never be within his control.

* * *

If only it was that simple, Joe thought later that afternoon as he stared at the very conference table in front of him. Caroline sat next to him, quiet and deep in thought, but he still found her presence disturbing. He wasn't able to concentrate on the meeting.

What was her Conference Table fantasy? Did she want to hide underneath it during a meeting and screw like rabbits? Or use it as a stage for a strip performance?

Joe's body clenched as his overly active imagination considered each fantasy in loving detail. He could see Caroline oiled to within an inch of her life, wearing pasties and a thong. His cock rose at the thought of her slithering around the conference table before she gave him a personal lap dance.

"Then that's it," Huang said, signaling the end of the meeting.

The bumping of chairs and rustle of papers sounded loud to Joe. He closed his pen with agonizing slowness as people walked around him and exited the room. He had to wait for his erection to diminish before he even tried to get up from his seat.

When he saw no one left, Joe decided it was safe to leave the protection of the table. The sound of the lock turning ricocheted in the quiet room. Joe turned and saw Caroline leaning against the door.

He swallowed and his mouth went dry. He was in trouble. He knew he wasn't strong enough to resist her.

It didn't matter that she wanted to purge him from her mind. It was irrelevant that her goal hurt like hell. The desire sparkling from her eyes resurrected the fantasy she had so easily destroyed.

"Hi, Joe," she said, breaking the tense silence. The seductive purr was more dangerous to his senses than any heart-melting smile. "I haven't been able to talk to you today."

"Yeah?" He leaned back in his chair, trying to play it cool. "What's there to talk about?"

She paused with uncertainty. "You know, it's okay to discuss us. I'm not hiding our relationship to my coworkers."

Yeah, he'd found that out at lunch. It sounded like she discussed nearly everything with her friends. "Since it's only going to be a one-night stand," he reminded her, "I don't see a need to discuss it."

"I've been thinking about that," Caroline said as she walked toward him with a feminine confidence that made his cock thicken. Joe dragged his attention away from her curves and kept his focus on her face, which offered a different kind of danger. "I might have been hasty in declining your invitation."

"Is that right?" Often. Frequently. Round the clock. Mia's advice had quickly become his mantra. He bet it guided Caroline as well.

"Yeah, that's right." Caroline leaned her hip against the conference table. If he wanted to, he could grab her. Pull her on his lap. Take her. But that wouldn't make her his, so he kept his hands on the armrests.

His chest tightened as Caroline sat down at the table and crossed her legs in front of him. He saw the promise of skin and silk. The rasp of her nylons scraped his sensitive nerves.

He wanted her so much. He wanted to live out his conference table fantasy. But if he gave in again and again, how strong would he be when she finally got over him?

Of course, he could try to stay permanently in her mind. Could he make her stay awake at night craving for him? Tease her, torment her until all she could do would be to live, breathe, and do nothing but think of him? Basically, give her his life.

Joe felt the smile tugging the corners of his mouth. The irony was not lost on him.

He could lose everything with that kind of strategy. He

wasn't sure if it was worth the gamble because he wanted her above all else. All of her.

However, he was aware that he was going to lose her if he didn't do something about it. He also knew he wasn't going to take what he could get. He might have grabbed it with both hands this morning, but everything had changed.

"You want more than a one-night stand?" he asked as he reached out and cupped her leg. The moment his hand brushed the silk, he remembered why it was such a bad idea to touch her. It was like playing with dynamite.

"What if I took you to my place during the day?" he asked as his fingers glided to the back of her knee, one of her most sensitive spots. He smiled as her leg twitched. "What if we didn't even make it out of the parking lot? Would you like that?"

"Yes," she whispered harshly and licked her lips.

He dipped his hand under the hem of her skirt. "And if I'm overwhelmed with desire for you here at work, what if I cornered you in your office? Would you want that?" He skimmed her inner thigh. "Would you want me?"

She parted her legs. "Yes."

"Even now," Joe said in a growl as he rose from his seat. He cupped her damp panties and his cock twitched in response. "If I wanted you right now, I could lay you down on this table. I could take you right now."

Caroline closed her eyes and tilted her head back. "Yes," she whimpered.

He rubbed her through her panties. The friction created a seductive heat. He wanted to tear the barrier away, but that didn't figure in his plans. Yet. "I'll keep that in mind," he whispered in her ear.

"Ye-huh?" She jerked her head up. Her eyes were blurry with desire as she stared at him.

"Last night was all about you and your fantasies." His fingertips trailed along her seam. When she shuddered, he pressed down harder. "This is about mine."

She clamped her legs against his hand, keeping him captive. "I don't understand. You said—"

"That all I wanted was you in my bed one night." His thumb sought and found the point that made her moan, long and deep. A fine sheen of sweat appeared on her skin. "Yeah," he continued with a satisfied grin, "but like yours, my fantasies grew. I want more."

"More?" She bucked against his hand.

"I want you all the time," he admitted, pressing the heel of his hand against her mound. "But there are a few fantasies that drive me wild. Dreams where I take you . . . claim you . . . here in this very building."

"Like now?" she asked in a daze.

"Yeah. And I'm going to act out every one of them with you. No warning, no nothing. Just be ready for me." Unable to decide if he was crazy, a genius or perhaps a crazy genius, Joe walked away. He unlocked the door and left without looking back.

"Artemis, what am I going to do?" Caroline asked later that day in the women's restroom. She studied her reflection in the mirror with a critical eye and flipped her hair behind her shoulder. "I'll never know when he's going to just take me."

"What are you complaining about?" Mia called over the water gushing from the faucet. "It sounds very exciting."

"I don't want exciting," Caroline wailed. She couldn't believe she just said that, but it was true. "I want to have my fill and walk away."

"Yeah," Artemis said as she wiped her hands on the rough brown paper towel. "You're going to have trouble forgetting about him when you keep wondering if this is going to be the next moment."

"Unless he's just playing with you," Mia suggested as she turned off the faucet. "Maybe he doesn't want you anymore, but this is his way of letting you down easy."

The possibility sliced through her. Caroline struggled for her next breath as she stared at her stunned expression in the mirror. "I hope not," she finally said.

"Joe wouldn't do that," Artemis said decisively as she tossed the paper towel into the trash. "If he didn't want you, he would say so."

Caroline agreed with Artemis's opinion, yet her friend knew Joe on a professional level. When adding sex to the equation, people act differently.

"But now I'm going to have to make that recipe of yours in bulk," she complained under her breath as she tweaked the lapel to her suit jacket. "I'm going to have to wear it constantly. And, no offense, but it's not the best-smelling potion."

Artemis did a double take. She looked at Caroline in the mirror. "Wear?"

"I hope it doesn't stain fabric," Caroline said. "That would be a bummer, because I found this fantastic dress at Nordstrom's the other day. Joe would keel over if he saw me in it."

Artemis was suddenly in front of her and blocked her view from the mirror. "What do you mean, 'wear'? You were supposed to drink it."

Caroline froze. Was she kidding? "Drink it? That stuff is vile."

"Hey, I updated the recipe with club soda to cut the taste," Artemis said defensively. "But it's not poisonous. You know that." She tossed her hands up in the air. "You're an aromatherapist, for goddess's sakes."

"What are you guys talking about?" Mia asked, her voice steeped in suspicion.

Caroline searched her memory. "The recipe never said anything about ingesting." She knew it hadn't because she was very careful with the directions. She even did the corny chant. Ice formed in the pit of her stomach at the possibility that all had not gone as planned.

"Oh, dear. Caroline." Artemis used a tone people used when speaking to the slow-witted. "Do you remember the name of the recipe?"

Mia was suddenly at their side. Her gaze went back and forth between the two friends. "Are you guys talking about what I think you're talking about?"

Artemis decided to answer for her. "It's Potion Spritzer #9." She gave an expected pause.

"And that's what I did." She mimicked how she had sprayed the potion on her using an atomizer. "I spritzed it all over me."

Artemis cupped her hands on Caroline's shoulders. She closed her eyes and shook her head. "No, that's wrong. Spritzer as in *wine* spritzers. Otherwise it doesn't work."

Chapter 5

"Nooo." Caroline's voice shook with horror.

Artemis winced, preparing herself for a cataclysmic explosion. "Yes."

"That means he saw . . ." She clapped her hand over her mouth as her stomach rolled. "Everything."

"Did he say anything about it?" her friend asked cautiously with her lip caught between her teeth.

Caroline wasn't prepared to think about it. She didn't want to remember all the stupid, goofy things she did. "I don't know."

"Maybe he didn't notice," Mia said. Her forehead crinkled with confusion as she tried to keep up with the conversation. "What do you think he noticed?"

"Maybe he didn't care," Artemis said hopefully, determined to shed the best light on the situation.

Caroline thumped her chest with her hand. "I care. I can't believe this. What am I going to do?"

"I don't know," Mia said, "but could someone tell me what's going on?"

"Maybe you can still use the spell. I'll walk you through it," Artemis offered.

"But the damage has already been done." She turned

and rested her forehead on the towel dispenser. The chrome felt cool against her clammy skin.

"Excuse me," Mia butted in. "You gave her a spell?"

"That's not the point," Artemis muttered.

Mia placed her hands on her hips. "Let me rephrase that." Her voice raised an octave. "You gave her a spell and you won't give me one?" She punctuated the question with a stomp of her foot.

"We will discuss that later," Artemis said in a threatening sing song tone.

Caroline lifted her head and took a deep breath. "I have to go. Go lock myself in my office and think." And she might not leave her office ever again, she thought.

"It's going to be okay," Artemis said and patted her shoulder. "Mia and I will put our heads together and come up with something."

Caroline nodded and hurried out of the bathroom. She needed to be by herself. She needed to hide. Needed time to transform into the ultimate bombshell.

The one time she lowered her guard . . . Caroline blinked back the tears of humiliation as she strode down the hallway. There she was, thinking it was safe, and whammo! So not the case.

Worse, she was goofier than ever. Caroline smacked her palm against her forehead. Why had she thought she could enjoy the freedom with no repercussions?

This could *not* be happening, she decided as she walked by the vending machine alcove. When she faced rejection from Joe, she didn't want it to be about her "inner geek" as Artemis so aptly put it. She could cope with any other reason. Rejection of any kind would be painful, but that one reason would devastate her and she didn't think she would have the strength to put herself back together again.

Caroline yelped as she felt two hands snag her by the waist. Her arms and legs went rigid as she was yanked into the alcove. "Jiminy Cricket!" The childhood cuss word tore from her lips before her mind formed something more appropriate for the occasion. And for the bombshell.

Without warning, she faced Joe Hatcher and her back was against a humming vending machine. "Excuse me?" Joe's eyes crinkled with amusement. "What did you say?"

She knew her cheeks were turning red. The heat singed her skin. "Never mind that," she said primly and pressed her hands against the machine. "What are you doing?"

"Didn't you hear me this morning?" His hands skimmed her hips. "Anytime. Anywhere. And I have lots of fantasies." He wagged his eyebrows.

"Here?" She looked around at the coffeepots and soda machine. Her gaze held at the entrance that had no door. Offered no privacy. "Now?"

He raised her leg and hooked it over his hip. "Here," he repeated huskily as he reached for her other leg. "Now."

Her heart tripped and heat blossomed in her pelvis, but she knew it was a bad idea. "We can't do this," she hissed, glancing over his shoulder at the entrance. "Anyone can walk in."

"Better take me fast." He lowered his head and staked his claim with a kiss. Her last coherent thought was *Who was taking whom?*

His mouth was insistent and dominating. She couldn't deny him anything even if she wanted to. His taste was addictive. Urgency swirled around her as she matched his kisses and drew his tongue into her mouth.

Joe pulled away from her, his ragged breath matching her uneven pulse. "I want to take you right now. Against this machine," he confessed, resting his forehead against hers. His chest rose and fell rapidly. "But you're right. This isn't the place for it."

"No, it isn't," she whispered, but at the moment, she really didn't care. Her body was too busy screaming for completion.

"Can't risk people walking in." He stepped away from

her with great reluctance. "We should finish this tonight at my apartment."

Apartment? Warning signs flashed in her mind. If she accepted, Joe would get an unexpected private showing of *Revenge of the Nerds*. "I can't."

"Okay," he shrugged and unhooked her legs from his hips. "If that's what you want. I guess we'll both go blind from frustration."

"Joe!" She suddenly understood. He was blackmailing her with sex. If she wanted it, wanted him, she would have to accept his terms. "That's it. You have pushed me too far. We are through."

"Because I wouldn't take you against a vending machine?" he asked, resting one hand next to her head.

"Yes." She shook her head. "What? No."

Joe clucked his tongue. "You don't want more than a night, and then you do. You don't want me to take you in a public place, and then you do. Let me know when you do make up your mind."

"My mind is made up." She tilted her chin and looked him in the eye. "All I wanted was a one-night stand."

His eyebrow soared. "Purge me from your mind already?"

Caroline gasped. "How do you know about that?" She had a sickening feeling that she wasn't going to like the answer.

"I heard you this afternoon at lunch." He replied lightly, but the gleam dimmed from his eyes. "I was in the booth behind you."

What had she said? She couldn't remember. How much did he know? "It's not as bad as it sounds."

"If I heard correctly," he said, his expression growing harsh, "you wanted to have sex with me so that you weren't inconvenienced by your fantasies."

She cringed. "Okay, it does sound bad."

"And just what is wrong with me?" Joe's expression

darkened. "Why am I not 'relationship' material? What did I do that made you decide this?"

He was off the mark. Joe would make a great boyfriend, the best husband. Her chest squeezed with the knowledge that he wouldn't be hers. Because she wasn't made of the right stuff. "It's not you, it's me."

Joe rolled his eyes. "Right. I think I deserve a better answer than the standard kiss-off."

She gnawed on her lip. "What all did you hear this afternoon?" Caroline asked cautiously.

"Why?" His green eyes narrowed into slits. "What else do you have to hide?"

"Nothing." Except for the nerd thing and the magic potion gone wrong. "Well, I don't know how to explain this, but when I'm around you, I don't like the way I am."

He stepped back as if she had surprised him with a punch. "I bring out the worst in you?"

Caroline frowned. She wouldn't exactly phrase it like that. "More or less."

Hurt shimmered in his eyes. "I'm not good enough for you?" he asked hoarsely. "Okay, I see."

"No!" How could he think that? It was the other way around. "That's not it at all!"

"Then what?" His nose flared with impatience.

"When I'm around you, I turn into a . . ." Fear gripped her throat. If she told him, there was no turning back.

"A what?" he prompted her. "Sex maniac?"

She glared at him. "A nerd."

Joe gave her a startled look before amusement flared into the green depths. He pressed his lips together. She could hear him choking on a laugh.

Caroline folded her arms across her chest. "It's not funny," she told him. "I don't find it the least bit humorous."

"I bring out the nerd in you?" he asked in disbelief. "That wasn't what I was going for."

"I don't want to be a nerd," she said in a low voice. "I

thought I eradicated that entire element from my personality. And then you,"—she pointed an accusing finger at his chest—"started showing interest in me."

She could tell that Joe was trying really hard not to laugh. She could also tell that he was losing the battle. "What's wrong with being a nerd?" he finally asked.

"Are you serious?" What planet was he from? "No one likes them." She ticked off the reasons with her fingers. "They aren't attractive. They are not lovable."

He shook his head. "You're wrong."

No, she wasn't. She was an expert on the matter. "Believe me," she said coldly, "nerdy is not sexy."

"Do you know what you were doing when I first decided I wanted to ask you out?"

If his indulgent tone didn't raise her hackles, the leading question definitely set her teeth on edge. "I'm almost scared to ask."

"You were in your car in your parking lot." Tenderness gleamed in his eyes as he remembered. "I could hear "Copacabana" playing full blast even though the windows were rolled up."

"Oh, no." She covered her hot cheeks with her hands. "Tell me I wasn't."

"And you were dancing some sort of rumba to the music." He stretched his arms out and shook his chest.

Caroline looked at him with a mix of dismay and skepticism. "This made you think, 'Oh, wow, that woman is so hot'?"

His smile was wide and seductive. It invited her to join in the fun. "No, I thought it was cute."

"It's not cute." She grabbed the lapels of his jacket. "There's a dark side to nerds. It isn't pretty."

He covered her hands with his. "I'm going to disagree with you on that."

"Joe . . ." Her fists tightened against the dark fabric, "You have no idea—*no* idea—how bad it can be."

"I'll take that risk."

She sighed and dropped her hands from his jacket. He didn't understand. "I'm not sure if I can."

The angles of his face tightened with disappointment. "Nerdy doesn't turn me off," he said, "but cowardice does."

Caroline's eyes widened. "I am *not* a coward." It had taken guts to survive her childhood. It required a certain level of daring to reinvent herself. No one could rightfully think she lacked courage.

"Yeah, you are. I made love to you and you throw it back in my face and tell me you only wanted a one-night stand." His stark expression gave her a glimpse of the pain she had caused him. "I put myself out there and you kept rejecting me."

She opened her mouth, but he placed a silencing finger against her lips.

"I have fallen for you and you want to purge me from your mind," he confided. "I keep taking chances with you, never knowing if I'm going to achieve my dream or get shot down for trying."

Her eyes glistened with tears. "Joe."

"No." He clearly didn't want to hear another word. "No more. This time you have to take the chance. Otherwise it isn't worth it." He turned and headed for the door. "When you decide to take the risk, you know where you can find me."

How long was it going to take for her to make a move? Joe went through his mail, viciously slicing the envelopes with his letter opener. It had been two days, but he thought she would have done something by now.

And the longer she waited to make the next move, the least likely she was going to take a chance. He slit open the next envelope savagely. She obviously thought he wasn't worth the risk.

He flicked a glance at the letter, but Caroline was in the forefront of his mind. As she had been since he had given the ultimatum. Joe sighed, crumpled the letter with more force than necessary and threw it in the waste can.

He didn't know how he was going to live with Caroline's decision. How was he going to look at her and know he could never touch her? He sighed again and opened the interoffice envelope. A small rectangular piece of paper fell out.

Not paper. He frowned as he realized it was the back of a photograph.

Joe flipped it over. His heart stopped as he stared at what was clearly a younger Caroline. A very nerdy Caroline.

Glasses that were much too big for her face slid precariously down the slope of her nose. Were the lens tinted purple or was that just bad lighting? He honestly couldn't tell.

He noticed that her black hair looked like a survivor of a perm that wouldn't die. Caroline's blemished skin seemed ghostly pale—probably because of the neon-orange clothes. If the Scholar Quiz T-shirt couldn't leach the color out of her complexion, it at least tried to swallow her petite frame.

But he could look past the braces and see the smile. Joe smoothed his thumb against the image. Her smile was wild, confident and brave. Despite it all. Or maybe because of it.

This was what she was afraid of becoming? This was how he made her feel? His hand shook as he felt powerful and weak at the same time.

And she was willing to take a chance on him. Hope swelled his battered heart. This was her risk.

Joe bolted from his seat and slipped the picture into his shirt pocket. He had to find Caroline. She needed to know that she couldn't scare him off. That he was worth the risk.

But after a quick search in all the usual places, he couldn't find her. Had she left for the day? He considered the possibility as he stormed down the steps. Had she been unable to handle his response, no matter what it happened to be?

Joe raced past the opened door of the graphics department in the basement. One glance and he could tell she wasn't there. The copy center in the next room with its humming machines proved fruitless. He hurried past the mail room.

He screeched to a halt when he saw the familiar figure in front of the wall of mail slots. Caroline stood tall and proud, regally beautiful as she went through the mundane chore of sorting through a handful of her mail.

Joe studied her mouth, the lush lips that offered him so much pleasure. Spawned so many fantasies. The wild smile in the picture was a rare sight, but he recalled seeing it a few times during that one-night stand. He wondered if he could draw it from her every day.

Approaching her quietly, Joe noticed the mailroom was empty. When he was right behind Caroline, he reached around her. She stiffened from the unexpected move. When he held the picture in front of her face, her sharp intake of breath echoed in the room.

He leaned down and whispered in her ear. "Like I said, I think you're cute."

"And I think you are seriously demented." She reached for the picture, but he kept it out of her reach.

Caroline turned to face him. "I need the picture back. Please," she added with a determinedly polite smile. Her gaze worriedly returned to the incriminating photo.

He tucked the picture back in his shirt pocket. "I'll keep it safe," he promised. And he meant it. While he thought it was cute, he knew what that picture represented to her.

Caroline bunched her hand, fighting the urge to go after the photo. "I don't want anyone to see it, even by accident."

"I'm keeping it close to my heart."

She looked at him as if he had lost his mind. "Why would you want to do that?"

"Because it's you." He circled his fingers around her wrist and brought it to his mouth. He placed a gentle kiss against the pulse point. "It's a picture of the woman I love."

Her eyes glowed from his words. He knew that one day she would trust him enough to say the words back to him. He could be patient, now that he knew it was inevitable.

"That is of the woman I used to be," she corrected. "I'm not that anymore."

"It made you what you are today." He leaned into her. "Do I really make you feel like that?"

"Worse. You have no idea."

"Good." His mouth grazed her lips.

"No, it's horrible!" she exclaimed. She glanced down at his pocket. "Give that back to me."

He stepped away as she lunged. "Don't you think you make me feel like that?" he asked, avoiding another swipe of her hands. "Maybe even a hundred times more."

She scoffed at the idea. "I doubt it."

"I'll have to show you my yearbook picture. But it's not leaving my condo. You'll have to come over for dinner tonight."

The corner of her mouth tilted into a smile. "You don't have to show me your yearbook, Joe. I'll show up for dinner anyway."

"Better pack an overnight bag while you're at it," he suggested, never one to rest on his victories. "I'm not letting you out of bed so quickly this time."

"I'll hold you to that promise," she said as she made another lunge for his pocket.

Joe neatly sidestepped her but collided against the mail cart. He reeled and before he knew it, he had landed in the giant linen basket. Envelopes and postcards flew around him like feathers as he stared dazedly at the overhead lights.

"Joe!" Caroline peered over the cart. "Are you okay?" she asked, trying hard not to laugh.

He patted his shirt pocket, making sure her picture was safe. Paper crunched with every move he made. "Yeah. Care to join me?"

To his surprise, Caroline placed her hands on his thighs and slowly crawled down the length of his body. Her hands clung to his shoulders as her feet dangled outside the cart. The short skirt she wore slid down to the tantalizing curve of her bottom.

"Did I ever tell you about my mailroom fantasy?" she asked as a wicked gleam in her eyes turned him inside out.

"No." He threaded his fingers through her hair and brought her lips to his. "Tell me how it goes."

And don't miss Erin McCarthy's latest book
MOUTH TO MOUTH,
also available now from Kensington . . .

"He's not going to show."

Russ Evans didn't even spare fellow detective Jerry Anders a glance, his eyes trained on the coffee shop across the street and the woman inside sitting alone. "Ten more minutes."

Jerry didn't protest, but Russ felt him shift in agitation, the heels of his shoes crunching in the hard-packed snow. Russ knew Jerry was cold, because he was, too. Hell, cold was an understatement. His nuts were completely numb. January winds were creeping in under his nylon jacket, and his fingers were stiff wrapped around the binoculars he was using to watch the door of the coffee shop.

But discomfort was part of the job, and he wasn't going to be hanging his badge up anytime soon. In fact, he loved being in Special Operations, got a kick from the watching and the waiting and the thinking—cold nuts or not—because in the end there was nothing like slapping the cuffs on slimeballs.

"He's standing her up."

Thoughtful, Russ scanned the nearly deserted parking lot. Nothing. Their target, petty con artist and first-class bastard Trevor Dean was nowhere to be found, and it didn't add up. There was no reason to think Dean had figured out the cops were waiting for him, but it wasn't like Dean to pass up a chance to meet a woman.

Women were Dean's source of income, and he liked to live well beyond his means.

"Not his usual type, is she?" Russ took another hard stare at the petite woman sitting in the shop with a cup of coffee in her hand, a thick pink scarf wrapped around her neck. The view of her face was obscured by the frosty glass, the coffee steam, and the rich blond hair that fell over her cheek, but Russ could see enough to feel the prickles of intuition tripping up his spine. Something was off here.

"You mean she's not butt-ugly?" Jerry cupped his hands and blew into them.

Russ laughed. "No. Look for yourself." He handed over the binoculars. "And Dean's women aren't ugly, they're just . . . plain."

"Just plain ugly, maybe." Jerry studied the blonde. "But this one's not bad. Good hair, tight sweater—I'm liking it. Hey, she just licked her lips, did a little nervous tongue thing. Do that again, honey."

"Glad you're enjoying yourself." Russ stamped up and down a little to get the blood flowing in his legs.

"Well, my pants are warmer anyway."

"But don't you think it's strange that this woman looks so different? I don't like it when a con changes a pattern without reason. He's been going after plain women, earning their trust. Letting them think he's in love with them, then stealing everything they've got—and it's been working. That we know of, he's hauled off a hundred thousand bucks so far. And there's probably been more. So why do anything different?"

Binoculars still stuck to his eyes, Jerry murmured, "Maybe this one isn't for business. Maybe this one is just for pleasure."

Russ hauled himself off the brick wall of the bookstore

and pitched the cigarette he'd been holding down into a snowdrift, where it sizzled. He'd been hanging onto the thing just in case they were spotted. It would look less suspicious, like he'd just stepped outside of the store for a smoke. He dug a cinnamon disk out of his pocket, unwrapped it, and popped it into his mouth.

Crunching on his candy, Russ said, "Like a girlfriend, huh? A real one?" He bent over and picked the butt back up once it stopped burning and dropped it in the pocket of his jacket. "You could be onto something, Anders."

"What can I say? I'm a deep thinker."

"Bullshit." Russ grabbed the binoculars off of Jerry's face. "Pick your tongue back up off the ground before it freezes to the concrete."

"So if Dean's got a girlfriend, why's he standing her up?"

"Because you can stand up your girlfriend. 'Sorry babe, I got held up' and all that shit. You can't do that with a woman you're trying to con." You don't piss off the meal ticket.

Jerry snorted. "Maybe you can stand up your girlfriend and get away with it, but Pam would rip me a new one if I did that. Of course, you don't got a girlfriend, because nobody will put up with your ugly mug."

"I don't have a girlfriend because I don't want one. I'll stick to casual sex. You can keep all that other crap that goes with a relationship." Russ didn't have time for it. Between his job and raising his little brother, Sean, he barely had time to go to the john. And he'd never met a woman yet who didn't make things more complicated than they needed to be.

"You're a cold man, Evans. But someday you're going to get knocked on your ass by some woman and I'm going to be there taking pictures."

Russ only half-heard Jerry razzing him as he puzzled

over the blonde waiting for Dean. If this woman was Dean's girlfriend, was she in on the con? What did she know? And could she be coerced into talking?

Stuffing the binoculars in his pocket alongside the cigarette butt, he started across the street.

"Where the hell are you going?"

"Stay here a minute, Anders. I'm going in the shop, get a better look at this chick. I've got a feeling about her."

"Yeah, I just bet you've got a feeling," Jerry grumbled. "Fine, leave me out here freezing my ass off while you check out the blonde. I'm waiting in the goddamn car."

Russ grinned over his shoulder. "Don't be such a whiner. Jesus. If you're quiet, maybe I'll even bring you a coffee."

"Do that, Evans. So I can spill it on your lap."

The warm air from the shop hit Russ as he opened the door, enveloping him in the scent of coffee beans and chocolate. The bell announced his entrance and the spike-haired guy working the counter glanced over, gave him a head nod. "Hey, how's it going?"

"Good." Russ waited for the blonde to look up, but she didn't. She was reading a magazine, a strand of her hair wrapped around a finger and pulled across her lips.

She didn't look capable of theft. She looked sweet and innocent, her fleece scarf making her look like an overzealous Old Navy employee on her coffee break. But Russ knew looks were deceiving. He'd seen the most evil hearts lurking behind pretty faces.

His fingers were still frozen, so he went to order himself a coffee. Then he would feel the blonde out, see where she fit in this puzzle so he could track down Dean. The chalkboard menu was riddled with flavors and blends, iced and hot, mochas and javas and lattes, and he gave up trying to read it. "I just want a cup of coffee. Black."

The guy wiped his hands on his green apron. "What

kind of bean? You can pick from these." He pointed to the case of seventeen different bean flavors.

"Oh, Jesus Christ." Scanning the variety of French this, vanilla that, winter roast whatever-the-hell-that-was and hazelnut, he said, "Just give me something with no flavor. Something that just tastes like coffee."

The clerk smirked a little. "You know, there's a Perkins down the street. They have that bottomless coffeepot deal going on."

Wiseass. Russ was debating flashing his badge to scare the little punk when he heard someone call, "Russ!"

Startled, he turned to see the blonde rising from her table, a welcoming smile dancing over her face. "I'm so glad you made it, Russ! I've been really looking forward to meeting you."

What the . . .

Knock him over with a fucking feather, the woman knew his name.

Here is a look at
THE BEACH ALIBI
by Alison Kent
. . . available now from Kensington!

He couldn't believe it.

He abso-fucking-lutely couldn't believe this was happening. Not here. Not now. No way.

He'd prepped for this mission for weeks. He knew every way into this building, every way out. Windows, elevators, ducts, doors, all of it.

He'd wallpapered his workstation with blueprints and surveillance photos, for fuck's sake.

How the hell could he have missed the goddamn camera hidden in the goddamn wall clock?

Kelly John Beach averted his head, stared at his black, rubber-soled shoes, at the pine green and navy leaf pattern in the executive suite's carpet beneath, and ordered himself to *think, think, think.*

The camera was new. The clock hadn't been here earlier tonight. He'd scanned this office an hour after the cleaning crew had left, doing an electronic sweep while in uniform as building security.

There had been nothing—*nothing*—on that wall other than the portrait of the company's founder. That didn't change the fact that now, at 2200, there was. Or the fact that the position he was in was more than compromising.

It was neck-in-the-noose illegal.

The CD of Classified Spectra IT intel he'd come for was tucked safely into the vest strapped to his chest. Getting out of here wasn't going to be a problem. He'd simply reverse the trip he'd made coming in.

The trouble would come later.

Three minutes from now, he'd be ground level wearing street clothes. Give the cops another thirty, he'd be wearing handcuffs.

God-fucking-damn.

Sweat beaded on his forehead, rolled like Niagara Falls down his spine. His eyeballs burned. His temples throbbed. His heart was a fist-size red rubber ball clogging the base of his throat.

He had to get to the SG-5 ops center without hitting the street. The only way to do that was the subway at the Broad Street station. Then underground.

He hated going underground. He hated the dark. Hated the rats. Hated the stench of shit and decay and all the rotten crap he'd have to step in.

Right! He growled, grumbled, snorted. Now he was really not looking forward to the trip. But a man had to do what a man had to do, or so went the saying.

And so he did. Sucked it up, swallowed his own bullshit along with the red rubber ball, and walked out of the office like the fucking president of the U. S. of A.

"Slow it down, son. Slow it down." Hank Smithson gestured toward Kelly John with the stub end of a cigar tucked in the crook of his index finger. "You're not going to get this figured out by wearing a hole in the floor."

The older man could use his calming techniques all he wanted. Kelly John wasn't in any mood to be calmed or gentled or put out to pasture. Not when it looked like what he was about to be was put down.

He paced the SG-5 ops center's huge horseshoe workstation from his own desk to Tripp Shaughnessey's and back. Again and again and again.

"Easy for you to say." Kelly John stopped, sniffed. Christ, but he smelled like a freakin' sewer. "You aren't the one who screwed up."

It was more than screwing up the mission and giving Spectra the upper hand. It was letting down the others, exposing the Smithson Group.

Failing Hank.

Hank crossed his arms over his chest and rocked back on his boot heels. "Kelly, you did your best."

His best hadn't been good enough. Not this time. A hell of a hard pill to swallow considering the reason Hank had picked him to join the Smithson Group in the first place. "They had to know I was coming. That's the only way the timing of that camera install makes sense."

"They were protecting their assets," Hank reminded him.

A reminder that pissed off Kelly John even further when he thought of the source of the organization's millions. "Yeah, well, now they've got video proving how insecure they really are. And how stupid I really am."

Hank moved, blocking Kelly John's path, commanding his attention. "We'll figure it out, son. We'll figure it out."

"What's to figure?"

At Tripp Shaughnessey's offhanded question, both men turned, Kelly John glaring down at his partner where Tripp sat on the floor in front of his desk. "What the hell's that supposed to mean?"

Tightening the wheels on his upended chair, Tripp shrugged. "You're the techno whiz. Make your own video. Prove you were elsewhere at the time. Show them they only think they know what they're seeing."

"An alibi," Hank said.

Intrigued, Kelly John started pacing again. "That might work."

"And we all know who makes the best alibi for a man, right?" Tripp asked.

Something in Tripp's tone told Kelly John he wasn't going to like the answer. "Who?"

"A woman."

Please turn the page for a sexy sneak peek
at Nancy Warren's hilarious new Brava romance
TURN LEFT AT SANITY,
coming from Kensington in February 2005.

"Don't you think we'll end up more frustrated if we keep talking and it doesn't go anywhere?"

"Well, last night would have been too soon, but now . . ."

Now, what? He came up with an answer for her. "Now I've passed the Miss Trevellen School of Larceny and Good Manners?"

She laughed aloud. Out of her peripheral vision she could see that Gregory Randolph had the hood up now on Joe's car. How long did this disabling business take? She was in a cold sweat, gulping her cocoa like it was courage-giving whiskey.

Greg was bent over the open hood of the car, his white T-shirt gleaming against the darkness. Please let him get the job done quickly.

A computerized ping broke the strained silence in the office and Joe said, "Ah, my e-mail."

He started to turn his chair around to his computer, which faced the window, which looked out on a man screwing with his car.

She had to stop him. No time to think. She stuck her foot out and stopped the chair mid twirl.

"Emmylou, I need to get that," Joe said, an edge to his voice.

"But I need you," she said, hoping that her voice sounded husky with passion and not strained by panic.

He opened his mouth, no doubt to tell her to get a grip, or at least wait until he'd read his e-mail. She couldn't let that happen, so she launched herself at him, sloshing cocoa mug and all.

"Whaa—" he managed to say before her lips clamped over his.

Blindly she managed to get her mug onto the desktop so her hands were free, then she plunged them into his hair, making a human vise to keep his head from turning. She opened her legs around his and snugged up tight onto his lap.

It was a move born of desperation, and if he pushed her off him, which she was pretty certain he'd do, she'd end up sprawled on her butt all over the rug and when he turned around, he'd view more than his e-mail.

She expected to go sailing through the air and hit the rug ass-first. She expected outrage when he caught sight of Greg out there messing with his car. What she hadn't expected was that after a startled second of total stillness, Joe would kiss her back.

Oh, not just kiss her, but make love to her mouth.

His passion exploded around her and in her, sparking her own. She nipped at his lips, grabbed the back of his head to pull him closer, felt his mouth so hungry on hers, on her skin, his hands in her hair, on her neck, racing over her back.

". . . want you," he said and the echo of those words played over and over in her head. *Want you, want you, want you . . .*

Heat began to build in the three point triangle of nipples and crotch. If Dr. Beaver was right, she had a dandy little electrical circuit running between those three hot spots.

He moaned with hunger, or maybe that was her, hard to tell over the pounding of her heart.

He pulled at the buttons on her shirt, fumbling open the top one, and then the second, while she waited in a fever of impatience. She forgot why she was doing this, forgot everything but the fact that she needed this man and she needed him now. He got the rest of the buttons undone, not smoothly, but fast. Then he pushed the sleeves down her arms to her wrists, and stopped, so she ended up with her arms bound behind her, a circumstance he seemed to enjoy.

With some wriggling she could easily free her arms but he looked so pleased with himself she let well enough alone.

"I like you in this posture," he explained with a devilish glint in his eyes. The fatigue had vanished and he pulsed with energy. "Your breasts thrust forward, and your busy hands still. No bread baking, flower arranging, cookie cooling. All you can do is sit there and let me touch you."

"Oh, honey," he said, gazing at her breasts for a long moment.

She felt naked, exposed, helpless. With her arms back like that, her chest was pushed forward, right into his face.

"*Annnnyyya,*" she said, when he lifted a breast and brought his mouth down to kiss the tip. Her head fell back of its own accord so she would have overbalanced and fallen on her head if Joe hadn't slipped an arm around her back to steady her.

He sucked at the swollen nipple, flicked back and forth with his tongue and generally teased her until her entire body felt lust-engorged and needy.

He sucked gently and she pulled herself upright anxious to press her torso more firmly against his wonderful, magical mouth.

When she did she let out a cry that had nothing to do

with passion. Gregory had abandoned tools and was standing there in front of the raised hood of Joe's car staring at her with his mouth hanging open.

Since she remembered well enough watching Joe from the garden, and thinking he looked like someone on TV, she knew she must look like the star of a porno flick. but she hadn't planned on acting out *Emmylou Does Joe* for an audience of one.

Fool! Bad enough Greg was an utter failure as a criminal. Did he have to be a peeping Tom?